Mac's Choice

Terri Marie Pemberton

Published by Terri Marie Pemberton, 2024.

MAC'S CHOICE

First edition. August 6, 2024.

Copyright © 2024 Terri Marie Pemberton.

ISBN: 979-8227581532

Written by Terri Marie Pemberton.

Table of Contents

Chapter One

Kate

Shoot, I'm going to be late.

I pick up speed at the thought, rushing through the parking lot of the one and only grocery store in Frostown on Friday afternoon.

Mr. Grayson is my last errand of the day.

I just need to get in and out before I can answer the call of the weekend.

Not that my weekends are exciting. You can't have much of a social life when you have no friends.

No, it's my promise to Mr. Grayson prompting my rush. He's homebound after a stroke and sadly, he has no family to help so I do what I can for him.

The sound of a loud motor snaps my head up. It must be the new motorcycle club in town. I'm no expert on vehicles but even I recognize the distinct sound of those engines.

Even though the Broken Souls Motorcycle Club has kept to themselves since their move here six months ago, everyone in town knows who they are.

Obviously, they come to town, but from what I've heard their trips are limited to bars, restaurants, or the grocery store. I haven't seen them myself.

Resuming my mission, I grab a cart on the way inside while I mentally map my route through the store. It helps to know Mr. Grayson's shopping list by heart as I quickly make my way through the aisles. That is, until I'm stopped in my tracks by a brick wall.

Not really. The only brick walls here surround the building, not the center of the store.

But it sure feels like it.

A brick wall definitely doesn't have the strong hands currently wrapped around my waist. Nor does one elicit the spark of electricity coursing through my body.

I inhale a breath to steady my nerves but it backfires as an intoxicating blend of leather and sandalwood, with a faint layer of motor oil, overwhelms my senses. This brick wall exudes a deliciousness that immediately brings to mind thoughts of sweaty tangled limbs and heights of pleasure I could only dream of. My eyes take a slow journey up strong thighs encased in denim, to a wide chest straining the seams of a black t-shirt until I finally reach the face of the most attractive man I've ever laid eyes on.

My eyes about pop out of my head as I realize the brick wall I barreled into is the most handsome man I've ever seen in my life. He must be with the motorcycle club. If the vest thing-y he's wearing is any indication.

I take a step back and admire the view as his hands slowly trace across my stomach. The touch is sizzling even through the material of my shirt.

Short brown hair shaved close on the sides; the top is just long enough to make a woman long to run her fingers through it. The scruff on his face, perfectly framing full lips, is just short enough to see the sharply chiseled line of his jaw.

I'm sure he has the body to match one of the model's gracing the covers of the raunchy romance novels I devour. No doubt, he'll be the star of all my fantasies now.

"Hey, sorry I wasn't watching where I was headed." The slow grin accompanying his apology is as hypnotizing as his voice. Smooth and soothing.

A girl could get lost in both.

Of course, I'm no exception. His grin even silences my inner voice.

Entranced, I watch as his smile morphs into a smirk while he slowly eyes me up and down like he likes what he sees. I have no hope of controlling the heat creeping over my face.

His eyes roam my body, igniting heat in more than just my cheeks. My nipples harden at the intensity of his perusal. There's no hope of hiding my body's response behind the cups of my lacy bra.

The jerk knows exactly what he's doing to me.

Okay, I have no idea if he's actually a jerk.

But it is a little jerky to call me on my embarrassment. Even non-verbally.

And my inner voice is back online.

I might be shy but my inner voice is not. It's as outgoing as you could get.

With my shyness, most of those thoughts never pass my lips.

Thank God for that.

Breaking from my trance, I finally find my voice. "That's okay. It was really my fault. I wasn't paying attention."

Smirk still gracing that beautiful face, he holds his hand out to me. "I'm Mac."

I, of course, go back to staring at him like a mute, ignoring his outstretched hand. There's no way I could survive without self-combusting with skin to skin contact. If just the feel of his hands through my clothes is anything to go by, I'd go up in flames.

"Hey, Mac, we gotta go." I'm jarred back to reality when a beautiful brunette wraps her arm around his waist, saving me from my embarrassment, even as her eyes spark with curiosity as she introduces herself. "Hi, I'm Jade."

Her smile is friendly. If there's hostility, I don't see it.

"Nice to meet you, Jade. I'm Kate." My manners return with my attention off the hotness she's attached to.

I reach my hand out to her, bypassing his still extended offering. Even though I broke eye contact, it's impossible not to feel the heat of Mac's stare that continues to caress my face.

She makes no effort to hide her amusement at my blatant move. It's obvious she sees exactly what's happening to me. She probably witnesses this embarrassing scene on the regular.

"Mac, we're running late. The brothers will riot if we're not back with food and drinks soon."

My eyes – stuck on them like a pre-pubescent teen – catch her turning back to me even as she guides him away.

"Kate, it was nice meeting you. You should come by the clubhouse sometime. All that blatant testosterone in your face gets overwhelming. Us girls could use some friends in town." Her invite is as friendly as her smile.

I won't lie. There is no way I'll show up there on my own.

Not because I judge. I just know my limits. And a rowdy crowd of men is a hard no for me.

If the steamy books I devour are true, all the men will be hot.

I'll be tongue-tied as heck.

Reading about and imagining sexy times is much different than being faced with real-life hotness.

Not wanting to be rude, I stick with a non-committal smile.

That was my first encounter with the motorcycle club since they moved here. I'm confident I won't run into them again. At least not anytime soon.

A wave of relief washes over me that I won't be forced to relive my embarrassment.

I'm sure I'm not even a blip on their radar, forgotten as soon as they walked away. Wish I could say the same for myself. I'll relive those hot looks for the foreseeable future.

A warning from my phone snaps me back to the task at hand.

Shoot, time got away from me. I'll be cutting it close.

Moving on auto pilot, my thoughts inevitably return to the handsome biker. Even with my limited experience, it was impossible to miss the interest in his electric blue eyes.

I know I'm not ugly but I'm no comparison to the beauty attached to him. If the familiarity between them is any indication, he's the complete opposite of my shy self.

I finish shopping quickly then I'm rushing back out to my car, the unusual heat and humidity hitting me hard.

This year's August heat is stifling. I can feel my hair revolt against the control I thought I had on it. Even in the normally mild Tennessee summers, I have no hope of taming my wild brown curls.

I never did learn how.

Growing up, my father considered hair products trivial and unnecessary. Even as an adult, I still haven't figured it out. It's easier to just pile it on top of my head or pull it back in a ponytail.

Putting my run-in with Mac and Jade out of my mind, I finally set off to Mr. Grayson's on the other side of town.

My anxiety mounts as I think of all I have to do. My to-do list is way too long. Never seeming to shorten, it just continues to grow. I don't even notice the shops and restaurants passing by on Main Street.

Preparing for the upcoming school year while making time for my true passion – volunteering in the community – I have no time to meet new people.

Not that I could make new friends to save my life.

My strict upbringing makes that impossible. Growing up with the school Principal father and meek stay-at-home mother wasn't a recipe for an extrovert.

My extracurricular activities were limited to what my father approved of. Playing in the school band when all the other girls tried out for the cheerleading squad. Labeled a nerd for always making the honor roll.

Though I wasn't bullied, the combination of the two didn't really incentivize my classmates to befriend the principal's daughter.

I was okay with that. My focus was on getting out from under my father's roof. And rules.

Scholarships were my only option to accomplish that.

College me was much the same as high school me. Minus playing in the band.

My head was in my books. I had no desire to party.

The one time my roommate talked me into going to one, I embarrassed her when I stood awkwardly in the corner all night. What she didn't understand is that I honestly lack the ability to socialize. I wasn't a snob.

Unfortunately, that's how I came across.

At one point, a popular football player approached my commandeered corner. The handsome baller made a quick exit when my awkwardness became obvious. Staring up at him like a mute didn't invoke stimulating conversation.

The ability to engage in casual conversation eluded me.

Even though I wish it was different, I've accepted my lonely existence. The only constant in my life is my cousin April and she's even more introverted than me. Understandable when you learn her history. Adopted by my aunt and uncle when she was four, April was a silent girl with haunted eyes when they brought her home. Just when she adjusted to a happy home, my aunt and uncle were killed in a car accident. I didn't see them often, so I didn't suffer as much as she did. My father didn't agree with their affectionate raising of her, so we kept our distance.

With nowhere else to go, April came to live with us. She had three good years with them before suddenly losing her loving parents. I thought April would struggle in our strict household but she seemed to thrive on my father's rules.

That wasn't the case with my mother.

When I was sixteen, Mom decided she'd had enough of his rules and ran away with another man. Last I heard, she remarried and lives in Florida with her new family.

Good for her. She found her happiness. But she left April and me alone with a bitter man. Her leaving only served to strengthen his resolve to control his household.

April is the reason I'm back in Frostown. When my father died right after my college graduation, I couldn't stomach the thought of uprooting her again. The best thing for her was to move back into my childhood home so she wouldn't have to move again.

I break from my trip down memory lane, not wanting to be late dropping off Mr. Grayson's groceries. April is waiting for me for our Friday night dinner.

I run up the walkway to Mr. Grayson's, only to stop and stare when I reach the door. I may have overestimated my abilities, juggling the bags to find the lock to fit my borrowed key.

Triumphantly unlocking the door, I call out to let him know I'm here. "Mr. Grayson? It's Kate. I have your groceries."

He wheels around the corner with a smile and I can't stop the responding grin lighting my face. His warm greeting always melts my heart. Despite his limited social interaction, he doesn't let it get him down.

Once again, I wish I could do more. If I had a way to transport his wheelchair, I would get him out of the house.

"Kate, how are you today?" He asks.

"I'm good Mr. Grayson. Did you get a chance to sit outside today?"

He has ramps that allow him to roll his wheelchair to both the front and back porches.

"You know I prefer sitting out when you're enjoying it with me. At least then I know you're taking a break." He always worries that I'm not taking care of myself.

Another reason to love him.

He's like the grandfather I always wished I had.

Maybe if I had a loving grandparent growing up, my father's overbearing ways would have been easier to handle. Or at least softened him.

"I can stay for a few minutes but then I need to get home to April." Everyone in town knows she's my main priority.

Everything I do, I do for her.

"That's alright. I know you're busy. We can sit a spell on your next visit."

I agree with a mixture of guilt and relief and we chat while I put the groceries away. Once the last grocery is in the pantry, I give him a quick hug before leaving.

With a wave, I'm back to my car.

It's a short trip home in our small town. A drive I could make in my sleep. As I take the familiar route home, my mind wanders back to my run in with the sexy biker. My cheeks heat at the remembered heat in his eyes.

How I wish just once that type of rugged man was truly attracted to me.

Sadly, he's probably already forgot all about me.

***

I pull into the garage with a sigh of relief. Pushing through the door to the kitchen, I call out my cheesy greeting. "Honey, I'm home!"

A grinning April waits for me at the kitchen counter. "You're right on time. I made spaghetti and meatballs for dinner."

"Sounds delicious. Let me go change really quick." I hurry down the hallway to my room.

It still feels weird to call the master bedroom mine. When I first moved back into my childhood home, I couldn't bring myself to move into his room. Instead, I stayed in what had been my childhood bedroom.

April finally convinced me to convert it to an office when it became glaringly obvious we were cramped with leaving part of the house unused.

It was a great idea. We've both gotten good use out of the change. Her for school and me for keeping my volunteer activities organized. Plus, a place to do any work from my actual job if needed, but volunteering is my true passion.

I mosey back to the kitchen where a still grinning April places the last dish on the table. "You look great. All your hard work is really showing."

Glancing down, my inner voice agrees with her.

I do look pretty good.

The leggings and tank are more revealing than my conservative work clothes. It wouldn't do to be mistaken for one of my students. There's no need to worry about that in the comfort of my own home. It's not like anyone but April is going to see me.

These clothes highlight the positive changes in my body.

My New Year's resolution to get healthier has had the added benefit of a twenty-pound weight loss. That wasn't my main goal but I can't say I'm disappointed in the results.

Even though my inner voice agrees, my shyness is ingrained and I automatically wave away her compliment. "It's all the clothes. Not much I can hide in these."

She rolls her eyes in exasperation. "It's not polite to disregard a compliment. Just say thank you and accept it."

With an eye roll of my own, I do as instructed. "Thank you, April. Now let's eat!"

Every week, I look forward to our Friday night feasts. The rest of the week is dedicated to a balanced diet. Friday night dinner means I get to skip the lean meats and fresh fruits and veggies.

If I've learned one thing throughout the process, it is to not deprive myself. While it's okay to indulge, moderation is key.

Diving in, we spend the rest of the night catching up.

April's eyes light up as she catches me up on her week and her friend Aaron. Aaron is her childhood friend. The boy who befriended her when she moved in with us. He's the only other person with the ability to tempt her out of her shell.

Aaron has been April's rock over the past ten years.

Once the kitchen is clean, we move to the couch to catch up on trashy reality TV.

I enjoy one of my last quiet nights before school and football season starts next week. Just like every year, I dread my required attendance at the team's home games.

Pushing away thoughts of my upcoming suffering, I settle in for our shared guilty pleasure.

Chapter Two

Mac

After dropping the groceries in the kitchen, Jade and I head to the bar for some much needed drinks. Already, rock music thumps through the clubhouse speakers as bodies fill the clubhouse.

The two of us have a long history. We became fast friends when we met freshman year of high school. Even though we both joined the military, we went separate routes after graduation but we did manage to stay connected over the years.

Eight years into my career, a bullet wound unexpectedly forced my early retirement. When I was discharged from the Navy, she didn't let my surliness deter her when I pushed everyone else away.

My asshole behavior was no match for her determination as she fought to drag me out of the depression that sucked the life out of me.

Aside from my Broken Souls Motorcycle Club brothers, she's the only close friend in my life.

While I was out of the bottle, shaking the guilt over the loss of my brother in arms was much harder. Helplessness and guilt consumed me when my teammate and friend committed suicide after our failed mission.

Brian couldn't get over not saving our teammates. The guilt of surviving when so many were lost was just too much for him. Add in the debilitating injury he sustained and it was more than he could handle. A month after he returned stateside, his parents found him dead in his wheelchair from an apparent overdose.

The inability to save my friend, along with the end of my dream of serving my country, left me adrift with no anchor. I was at a loss. Feeling like I failed everyone around me.

Ryker, my commanding officer in the Navy, paid me a visit after his retirement. Seeing my obvious struggle, he invited me down to his motorcycle club in Louisiana. And then challenged me to consider joining during my visit. As President of the Broken Souls MC, he offered to sponsor me as a prospect.

I was still undecided about my future and figured I had nothing to lose if I gave it a shot. I took him up on his offer and haven't looked back since. The MC gave my life meaning again.

It was a no-brainer when Jade joined along with me.

Since then, we've hooked up here and there. There's a familiarity we don't have with anyone else but it's nothing more than scratching an itch when we're both horny.

Throwing back her drink, Jade drags me to the dance floor as a slow song starts pounding through the speakers. Wrapping her arms around my neck she uses her hold to pull my body flush to hers.

While I'm usually right there with her, tonight her sexy moves do nothing to ignite my desire.

Out of the blue, an image of the curly haired beauty from the grocery store pops in my head. Fantasies of pulling her close, losing ourselves in the hypnotic beat pounding through the speakers.

I have no doubt she would fit perfectly in my arms, imagine the shape of her perfect curves teasing me. Moving close, then slipping teasingly away as her body sways seductively. The perfect little tease to rouse my desire higher and higher.

"Let's go to your room." Jade's moan in my ear pulls me from my daydream, normally it's something I wouldn't resist.

"How about a drink." I say instead of what I'm really feeling.

I'm just not into it tonight. The brunette from the grocery store lingering in my thoughts surprises me. Women don't typically take up residence in my head, more out of sight out of mind. That's just the way it's always been.

Before I can delve into what's different about this one, Ryker's voice stops us two steps off the dance floor. "Mac, we need to talk."

While Ryker commands the club with a firm hold, he's a true leader. He's earned the respect we have for him. And that includes every member of the club – both in our original charter in Louisiana and here in Tennessee.

The look on his face tells me all I need to know. My night's about to take an unexpected turn.

I drop Jade's hand as I join him at the bar. I curse at the seriousness on his face and call for a shot. The Prospect behind the bar slides it to me a minute later.

The whiskey burns down my throat to settle like a boulder in the pit of my stomach. I drop the empty glass on the bar before turning to Ryker. "What's up, man?"

My question is met with a scowl. "Not out here."

Shit, this isn't good.

Tilting his head to the large room where we hold club meetings. I follow without question. The respect I have for my Prez would have me following him through the gates of hell. No questions asked. Jade and the brothers right on my heels.

We do things differently than other clubs. The women are full members. That means including them in club business.

Ryker gets right to the point once we're all settled around the table. "There's been another overdose."

"Who was it this time?" Rocker's frustrated yell comes from across the table.

As the Enforcer for the club, he isn't a man I'd want to run into in a dark alley. Menacing as hell at six foot six, almost as wide as he is tall. His shaved head and full sleeves on both arms just add to the intimidation factor.

"A damn high schooler. Jonny Baker, he was a seventeen-year-old senior on the baseball team." Ryker's words hold equal frustration.

"Did he survive?" Rocker asks.

"No. This one didn't even make it to the ER. His parents found him when they got home from a trip yesterday. Already dead when they found him. This is the third overdose since we moved to town." Ryker's disgust with the entire situation is clear.

Curses echo around the room. None of us have any tolerance for the drug dealing that started not long after we set up the clubhouse right outside of town.

Ryker researched several locations when he decided it was time to expand from Louisiana. Ultimately choosing Frostown for the small-town vibe. We've held off really introducing ourselves to the community. Prez wanted to wait before we got out there more regularly.

Like a true leader, he gave all the club members a choice to follow him here. It was a no-brainer for most of us but some of the brothers stayed at our Louisiana charter. Wanting to stay close to the excitement of New Orleans, they're horrified at the thought of small town living.

Always the loudest in the room, Joker vents his anger too. "This bullshit needs to stop. What are we going to do about it?"

People assume his road name comes from his playful personality, his constant pranks. Misled by the laidback jokester, those people never see the calculating card shark just below the surface.

"Byte is looking into it." Ryker speaks over the brother's outburst. "For now, keep your eyes open. Report to me immediately if you see or hear anything. No matter how insignificant you think it is, I want to know about it."

"How are we supposed to do that? We've kept our distance from the townspeople." Joker never does know when to keep his mouth shut.

"Brother, that ends now. It's about time we introduce ourselves around town. Next Friday is the high school football team's first game. What better way to introduce ourselves than the team's home opener? This town is no different than any other small town. They live and breathe their school's colors. It's not hard to guess most everyone in town will be there."

The room explodes as everyone in the room tries to speak over each other. Brothers strategize the best way to entrench ourselves in the community. In a positive way of course.

We're not stupid, we know most of the townspeople fear us. It's the main reason why we've kept our distance. We wanted to give them time to adjust after we moved here.

"Some of the brothers are gonna ride up from Louisiana this weekend. Hopefully, showing up is all it'll take to run any dealers out of town." With that, Ryker bangs his fist on the table to dismiss the group of us.

"Mac." Ryker halts my trek back to the main room. "I want you to go see Byte. He's looking into a possible connection at the high school. We need to get a handle on this and stop the drugs running through this town. I trust the two of you to figure out a game plan."

"You got it, brother." While I appreciate his faith in my skills, I question if I'm really up to the task. I don't want to let him down.

I met Ryker not long after joining the Navy. We had each other's backs through years of deadly missions. He's counting on me to help Byte get to the bottom of this shitty situation.

I head out of the kitchen to join Byte for a long night of planning.

***

Hours later we've poured over all the available intel and there seems to be only one path forward. The problem is I don't like the option Byte is convinced is the only approach at this point.

"I don't like it." I'm not afraid to voice my concern with the plan.

"Man, there's no other way. You see the same thing as me." He continues to push me in the direction I really don't want to go.

Involving innocents is the last way we should be taking this.

"I want to get Ryker's opinion before we decide." I'm just not ready to agree to this yet.

Shooting Ryker a text, I sit back ruminating on the plan.

It only takes a few minutes for Ryker to knock before entering Byte's room.

"What do you have?" He gets straight to the point.

Byte jumps right in before I can. "There's a math teacher at the school that was working close with the student. Kate Grant, she's worked there since she moved back to Frostown a few years ago. Single. Doesn't seem to have much of a social life. We could use that to get close to her."

What are the odds the math teacher and curly haired beauty are one and the same.

Ryker turns a long look to me.

He knows me well enough to know I don't like this plan.

"What do you think, Mac? Should we approach her?" His tone gives nothing away.

"I think she might be able to help, but man you know how I feel about involving innocents." With a deep breath, I continue. "We have no idea who's dealing yet. What are we going to do if we put her in the crossfire without knowing who to protect her from?"

I don't mention my fascination.

How can I explain it when I don't even understand it myself?

"While I understand your concern, I don't think approaching her will cause any problems. At least see if she knows anything that could help."

There's nothing to do but agree, knowing it's the best I'm going to get at this point.

"Alright, Prez. I'll keep you updated." I agree.

Excitement wins out over hesitation as anticipation of seeing the wild haired brunette again surges like wildfire.

Chapter Three

Kate

Dragging myself out of bed at the crack of dawn Saturday morning, I question my life choices. Six a.m. comes way too early on the weekends.

If I didn't know how good I would feel after my run, there's no way I'd be forcing myself out of bed at this ungodly hour. Most days, that's enough motivation to get me moving.

Today is not one of those days.

Tiptoeing down the hall, even though there's no way I'll disturb April, I slip my feet into my running shoes at the front door. A tornado blasting through the house wouldn't wake that girl at this hour.

Our house sits in the middle of town. Only two blocks from Frostown High School and one over from Main Street.

If you thought the town got its name from the weather, you'd be wrong. Even though the winters deliver trace amounts of snow, the town is actually named after its founding family.

The Frost family settled in the area near the base of the Smoky Mountains in the 1800's. Their vision of building a successful distillery came to fruition and our little slice of heaven was born.

I could never imagine planting roots anywhere else in the world. The idyllic town is the perfect setting for the family I want.

A family that starts with finding a man. Unfortunately, I haven't found the time or courage to put myself out there for that.

But that's a worry for another day. The only date I have on my calendar is with the school this morning.

More accurately, a date with torture.

I start out at a brisk walk to warm my muscles. Hitting the end of my street, I speed up to a jog to get my blood flowing.

My route to the school takes me down Main Street. The only business with its lights on at this time of day is the new bakery that opened a few months ago. I've somehow resisted the urge to stop in so far.

On the opposite side of the street from yummy temptation is the church and antique store, both staples in this town for decades. The church was one of the first buildings that went up when the Frost family settled here.

As a little girl, my mom would treat us to weekly visits to the antique store. I'd get lost for hours exploring the unique treasures hidden on the shelves if she'd let me.

Nostalgia fades as I jog past. Running clears my mind, allowing me to mentally reset. My worries don't seem so bad when the endorphins are flowing.

There's something calming about starting my day in the peace and tranquility of the sleepy morning town. It sets a positive tone for the rest of my day.

When I arrive at the high school, I'm surprised to catch sight of a figure already circling the track around the football field. There's usually no one else around on Saturday mornings. Which is a good thing for me. It gives me the quietness I crave.

It seems my peace and tranquility will be interrupted today.

I jog onto the track when I realize I know that figure. Mac sets a mouthwatering scene with a quick pace around the track, soaked white shirt highlighting scrumptiously hard muscles. Thoughts of other more exciting sweaty activities invade out of nowhere.

In the six months they've been in town, I've never crossed paths with any of the bikers.

Of course, now that I made a fool of myself, I see him two days in a row. Just my luck.

I can't decide if that's excitement or dread pooling in my belly at the thought of talking to him again.

Deciding avoidance is probably the best way to go for my sanity, I pick up my pace and turn on my music. Then I start my circuit.

I'm in the zone. Everything else fades away.

That is, until I feel his presence approaching behind me. I'm not scared. Not sure why but I'm more embarrassed than anything.

Of course, he lapped me. I must look like an amateur to him.

Then to make matters worse, he obviously slows his pace to match mine. Chancing a glance up, I catch his panty melting smile, watch that sinful mouth form words. "Good morning." This close, I am bombarded by the vision of all those glorious muscles outlined by that plain white T-shirt.

One look into those mesmerizing blue eyes, I'm done for. Intoxicating. That's exactly what he is. The sight should be illegal.

My manners rear their ugly head, rudely pulling from my fantasy as I reach up to remove an earbud. "Good morning, Mac."

"You did catch my name yesterday." Hard to miss his pleasure when the dimples pop in his cheeks.

Of course he has dimples. Because he wasn't hot enough already.

With a ball cap pulled down to shade his eye and dimples chiseled into those cheeks, I have no idea how any woman resists this perfect picture of masculinity.

A blush creeps up my cheeks as my thoughts stray once again. Maybe luck is on my side and the early morning darkness hides it.

Yeah right. Like I'm ever that lucky.

I find my voice and answer his question. "I did. I'm surprised to see you here. I've never seen you running the track before."

"That's because it's my first time. I usually hit the roads around the clubhouse. Thought I'd try something new this morning." He says with a clear lack of exertion.

How is he not even breathing hard?

From the sweat staining his shirt, it's evident he's been out here a while. I feel like a sloppy mess next to him with my harsh breaths and sweat already beading my face and chest.

Although, the way his eyes keep dropping to my chest, he doesn't seem to mind me getting a little dirty.

Where are these thoughts coming from?

I know my inner voice can be outrageous but this is just out of control.

It must be him. The interest of a hot guy is definitely not something I can say I'm used to at all. The way his intense gaze watches me, eating me up. I feel naked. Exposed. Almost like he's imagining me without my clothes too.

I'm warming up in places I shouldn't be while exercising. My panties are damp. And not from my run.

His voice brings my attention back around to him. "Do you mind if I run with you?"

My manners won't let me refuse. "No, but please don't feel obligated. I don't want to slow you down. I'm definitely still building up my stamina."

"I don't mind going slow when it comes to something I want." He flashes another grin as his gaze trails slowly down my body. My stupid blush returns with his teasing.

I didn't need to see him in action to know the women must fall all over themselves for even a minute of his attention.

With those looks, you could be one of them.

I jog on without responding, the silence stretching between us. Surprisingly, it isn't uncomfortable, more so two people enjoying the peacefulness of the quiet morning together.

Rounding the track for our second lap, he breaks our companionable silence. "Did you grow up here?"

"Yes, my parents met at this school. They moved away for college but came back here to start a family after my father graduated. His parents left him the house I was raised in and he left it to me when he died."

"I'm sorry for your loss." There's sincerity in his words. Like he knows exactly how it feels to lose someone too.

"Thank you. It's been several years now and we weren't all that close. The hardest part was the house. Thinking of it as my own, you know?" I surprise myself with my honesty. "It wasn't until I started making changes that it really felt like it became mine."

"I can understand that. I'd probably feel the same way." He says.

"What about you? What brought you to our little town?" My curiosity overrides my shyness.

"Ryker wanted to expand the club and was looking for something different than New Orleans."

"Wow, that is a big change. Do you miss it?" It's incomprehensible why a man in his prime would want to move from a big city to our small town.

"Not really. It got old, ya know. I prefer the natural beauty of the area around here. And there was no question I would end up wherever Ryker landed."

Sounds like they're close. It's clear he has a lot of respect for his President.

I'm jealous. I've never had that kind of connection with anyone.

The easy flow of our conversation is a surprise. I answer his questions about things to do in the area. He admits he hasn't explored much.

"I've heard the ride through the mountains is beautiful, but I've never seen it myself." My admission is embarrassing.

Most of the activities I suggest would be better enjoyed with a partner. Because of my lonely existence, I either go it alone or drag April with me.

It is just not the same.

If he picks up on my embarrassment, he's gentlemanly enough not to let it show. "Maybe we could do that together."

For reasons I just don't understand, he seems genuinely interested in me. This easy conversation is the most comfortable I've had with an attractive man in my life despite the hot visuals of other sweaty activities that I just can't seem to drive out of my mind.

My five laps pass much quicker than usual. I'm soon slowing to a walk for my cool down. Mac shortens his stride to stay with me.

"That's it for me. I'm going to head home." I explain my slowed pace as I feel my heart rate return to normal.

Well as normal as it can in the face of his masculinity.

April should be getting up soon. I'm hoping to tempt her with a day at the lake. It's not often we get to spend time together. I want to enjoy these last few days before the school year starts. It saddens me that life will change for us after this year.

Mac's voice stops me in my retreating tracks. "Thanks for the company, it was a beautiful change of scenery. Much better than the sweaty brothers."

His smoldering blue eyes caress my body, igniting a blazing inferno in my core. Taking a chance, I glance back over my shoulder, catching his wink as he watches me walk away.

I almost trip over my own two feet at the heat in his eyes. At the way his sweat soaked shirt clings to all those hard muscles. Putting that perfect body on display.

Is it hot in here? Out here? Where am I even at? I have no idea. The man is *that* potent.

Could I really have attracted the attention of a man like that?

Not only is he the most attractive man I've ever met, with his lifestyle, he isn't hurting for female attention. I'm not so naive that I'm completely clueless to what goes on in a motorcycle club.

***

By the time I drag my tired body through my front door, I convince myself that I read too much into my interaction with Mac. There is no way a man that attractive would be interested in my boring self.

Thoughts of my confusing but companionable morning go up in smoke as I catch a whiff of breakfast cooking. I feel and hear my stomach growling as I enter the house.

It's a miracle!

April is up before I'm forced to take extreme action to wake her. I find her at the stove scrambling eggs, a plate of fruit sitting to the side.

"Good morning," I chirp, not even trying to hide the exhilaration from my morning run. And company.

I flash a grin at her grumbled "Good morning."

She might be up but she is definitely not feeling human yet. It's a fact she would much rather be in bed. So, her effort to make my morning a little easier is appreciated.

I sip a glass of orange juice as I watch her plate the eggs. "It's a beautiful morning. Do you have any plans for today?"

"No. Do you have something in mind?" She asks.

"I was thinking we could take a picnic to the lake. Maybe have a relaxing day before the summer ends and we both get busy." I fight the sad turn of my lips just thinking of the changes we'll soon experience. "I want to take advantage of the time we have left before you get busy with your senior year. Then before I can blink, you'll be heading off to college."

I'm not blind. I know April is hesitant about leaving home. With her limited friendships and difficulties in social situations, she's nervous to move away from her comfort zone.

I understand her feelings. I do. But it only makes me that much more determined to push her to expand her horizons.

Moving away from home, even temporarily, was something I'm glad I experienced. Even if I didn't take advantage of the full college experience, I had other experiences I wouldn't have had otherwise.

I push for her agreement. "So, what do you think? Want to spend the day at the lake with me?"

"Sure, give me thirty minutes to shower and get ready." She agrees.

"Sounds good. I need to do the same." Still high on endorphins, I head for the shower, excited for the day ahead.

Chapter Four

Kate

April and I bask in the sun after spending most of the day splashing around in the water. The sound of her laughter is bittersweet. I know these moments will disappear faster than I'm ready for. Nothing ever lasts forever.

After finishing our lunch, I sit back on the blanket in the heat of the sun.

"You've gotten a lot of sun today." Face raised to the sky, April states the obvious.

I can feel the warmth on my skin where the heat hits me. "It's probably about time to head home. I don't want to burn."

"Let's swim a little longer." Now that we're here, she doesn't want to leave.

We race back to the water, splashing like kids for another hour. The sun is starting to set when I walk out of the water.

"You're getting out already?" She complains.

"I'm turning into a prune." I show her my wrinkled fingers. "We should dry off and go home."

"I want to stay in the water a little longer." She's not giving up.

Not wanting to end our fun day with an argument, I grab a towel and leave her to swim a little longer. I watch her with a bittersweet smile as I make my way back to our picnic setup and start packing it all away.

The sound of approaching engines whips my head around to see a group of motorcycles pull in next to my car.

Self-conscious in my bikini, I'm berating myself for wearing something so revealing.

It's so rare to see anyone else in this secluded spot, I hadn't thought twice about putting it on this morning. Now I wish I'd picked something with more material.

Though from the revealing bikinis on the women climbing off the motorcycles, I don't have anything to worry about. Their suits, more string than anything, keep the attention off me.

The only familiar faces among the group are Mac and Jade. Jade waves as she climbs off the back of his motorcycle.

"Hey Kate!" Her friendly shout draws the attention of every single person to me.

I return her greeting even as envy courses through me as I witness her easy familiarity with the man that has taken up residence in my mind.

Has it only been a day since I met him? That can't be right, not with the way he consumes my thoughts.

Mac's eyes devour me, taking his sweet time running his gaze over my exposed skin. Logically I know it's impossible to *feel* that caressing gaze but tell that to the shivers rolling down my body.

Unaware of my flustered state, Jade leads the women to me while the men dismount their motorcycles. I'm distracted from Mac's intensity as I watch a petite blond, voluptuous redhead, and tall raven-haired woman follow her to where I sit.

She makes the introductions while pointing at each one in turn. "This is Josie, Raquel and Dana."

Of course, they're all beautiful in their contrast to each other. I'm feeling inferior in the face of their confidence. And beauty.

Oh, and let's not forget, string bikinis.

I definitely lack the confidence to put myself on display like that in public. Probably not in private either.

"Hi. It's nice to meet you." There's no way to hide the shyness of my greeting.

Friendly smiles grace the faces of Raquel and Dana. The slight frown on Josie's face takes me off guard. I wrack my brain wondering if we've met before. Maybe I've had an unpleasant run in with her around town?

Nothing comes to mind. Which makes her reaction even more confusing.

Mac's approach distracts me from that train of thought. His heated gaze still roaming my body makes me feel more exposed than the beauties surrounding me. Like there's no one else around.

Like I'm the most beautiful woman in the world.

"Running into you twice in one day, I'm a lucky man." His flirtatious words stir a slew of butterflies in my belly. His intense focus unnerves me. His gravelly voice arousing images of hot tangled bodies gliding together in the most erotic way.

"I don't know about luck, more like the consequences of life in a small town." I burn brighter, flustered at the ridiculousness of my words.

Once again, I'm so socially inept I have no idea how to flirt with a handsome man.

"Is that your sister?" Thankfully, Jade's question draws me from my embarrassment.

I completely forgot I'm not alone here. "No, that's my cousin April."

Frozen mid-splash, April sinks down to her neck in the water.

When I see her timidity overpowering her, any awkwardness I feel takes a backseat as I shift focus to getting her out of this situation.

"Hey April. Are you ready to go?" When my question is met with silence, I firm my voice. "April, I think it's time to go home."

When she still doesn't respond, I grab a towel and move to the edge of the water. "Sweetie, why don't you get out of the water and dry off so we can get home. Remember you said I've gotten a lot of sun today? I think you're right. I need to find some shade."

I wait patiently as she begins to slowly move toward me. She won't appreciate more attention if I try to rush her. I hand her the towel once she's in reaching distance and nonchalantly turn to finish packing our stuff.

Then I remember I'm in nothing but my bikini.

Oh God. I've been giving everyone an eyeful of my exposed body this entire time.

I quickly pull my white cover-up over my head to hide my near nakedness.

"Darlin' don't cover up on our account."

Not bothering to look up at whichever biker spoke, I focus intently on packing our things so I can get April out of here.

I don't notice Mac's approach until he kneels down to help me. Our eyes connect as we put hands on the picnic basket simultaneously. I release my hold as I get caught up in the interest he doesn't even try to hide.

"I can get it," I tell him.

Mac completely ignores my protest and carries the basket to my car. Gathering the bag and blanket, I rise to my feet and lead April that way.

Mac waits patiently at the trunk while I settle April in the car, opening the trunk when I'm close enough with the key. He takes the blanket and bag out of my arms and packs it all away before slamming the trunk closed. His gentlemanly actions surprise me.

"Thank you." My manners won't allow me to ignore his assistance even if I am doing my best to ignore the sparks flying between us.

Before my hand touches the handle of my door, Mac is there, invading my space, reaching around me to open the door for me.

"Are you sure you can't hang out with us?" The grin on his face is teasing but he seems serious.

"No, we've been here most of the day. I'll be burnt to a crisp if we stay any longer." His eyes take another leisurely roam over my body. Almost reflexively, like he just can't help himself.

"No, we don't want that happening to your beautiful skin." That constant grin, full of cockiness, fries my brain. And other parts of my body.

At his flirty words, my own gaze takes a slow exploration of his exposed skin. Without a shirt, all his hard tattooed muscles on display. My mouth turns to dust, my body overheats. My core pulses.

Unlike me, he doesn't seem too concerned with his own display.

And why would he be? His sun-kissed skin is the perfect backdrop for his multitude of tattoos. The play of muscles below his skin, the beautiful artwork dances in the sunlight.

Shaking off the brain fog, I reach out to close the door. Unfortunately, my momentum is stopped by Mac's hand still on the door.

That, of course, leaves me hanging out of the car awkwardly.

Mac hovers over me like temptation personified. One hand on the door, the other on the frame of the car, he cages me in. Blocking my escape. "How about a date then?"

"What?" I ask. I can't focus with him standing right in front of the door. Eye level with his happy trail. I have to clench my fingers on the door handle to keep from reaching out to trace it. To know if the hair is as soft as it looks.

"Go out with me." He presses.

His repeated request pushes my shyness right out the door.

"Why would you want to go out with me?" The ridiculous question shoots from my mouth before I can stop myself.

Oh God, did I really just say that? Let me disappear into the ground.

"Are you kidding?" My question seems to truly baffle him. "You're a beautiful woman and I'd love to get to know you better."

"Mac, come on! They aren't interested in hanging out with us." The petite blond, Josie I think, saves me from having to talk my way out of my awkwardness.

Her condescending tone breaks me out of my silence. The hatred on her face reaffirms my decision to leave.

"Go on. It's okay, you don't have to pretend with me. You all look like you'll have a great time without us." I prompt when he doesn't immediately move away.

The intensity on his face snaps my mouth shut quickly.

I'm aware of how rude I came across. I could have kicked my own butt for saying something like that.

A shake of his head clearly communicates his displeasure. After another silent minute, ensnared in his electric blue eyes because I couldn't look away if my life depended on it, Mac finally releases his hold on my door.

With an unfathomable sense of disappointment, I tear my gaze away. I quickly pull the door closed while starting the engine, thankful for the blast of the air conditioner on my heated cheeks. And other pulsing parts of my body.

I once again get caught in Mac's intense stare when I glance in the rearview mirror to see he hasn't taken his eyes off me. Like every time before, it takes effort to force my attention to the road in front of me.

I chatter senselessly to April to calm her during the drive home. Pulling into the garage, I fortify myself to forget my latest encounter with the sexy biker.

Determined to close myself off from the fantasy like the closing of the garage door behind my car.

Chapter Five

Mac

I turn a glare on Josie as Kate disappears down the road, no words needed to convey my irritation. Her jealousy is nasty whenever a brother shows interest in a woman outside the club. With today's scene, I see no way to avoid a conversation with Ryker about her.

Most of the brothers have backed off because of her behavior. Myself included. Even before meeting Kate, I've been clear with Josie that things are changing. I have no desire to continue a sexual relationship with her.

The ladies were busy spreading out the blankets while I was talking to Kate. They've set up blankets and chairs in a circle near the edge of the lake. Music blasts from Joker's Bluetooth speaker.

"Her cousin sure was quiet. Do you think she was scared or something else?" Ryker tosses me a beer while sharing his thoughts on the two women.

"I think she's just shy. She blushed when I made eye contact with her before she looked away." Joker throws in his unsolicited opinion. "After that, she wouldn't make eye contact with anyone."

"Josie needs to watch her mouth. She's been rude to every woman that comes around lately. She's getting out of control." I'm still pissed her attitude sent Kate running.

Add Josie's jealousy to my already mounting concern about pulling Kate into the investigation, I'm even more uneasy. Not only am I supposed to be getting close to her but I would be lying if I said she doesn't fascinate me. Maybe it's the thought of dirtying up her pristine appearance.

My dick swells just thinking of pulling her hair down. About wrapping those wild curls around my fist as my dick disappears between her plump lips. I know those curls are deceiving, appearing wild and uncontrollable. I have a feeling the strands will be like silk sliding through my fingers as I guide her mouth where I want it.

I shove off that erotic image before my dick swells to a full-blown hard-on. That would be impossible to hide in these damn shorts.

"Byte said her cousin is gonna be a senior at the high school this year. Said she became her guardian when Kate's father passed away and apparently, they're close. From what he saw of their social media, neither get out much." Ryker says what I already know.

I've read Byte's file front to back. Multiple times. They're both squeaky clean. If there is something shady going on at the school, my gut tells neither Kate nor April knows anything about it.

"I don't think they're involved. If they can help us, I doubt they even know it. They may not realize it but if they do, we'll figure it out. They might need the club's protection."

I know my Prez, he isn't going to hang two innocent women out to dry. He wouldn't be the leader we all respect if he did.

"The club will protect them if it comes to that." Ryker's words are the reassurance I need.

If I'm going to intentionally involve one or both of the sisters in our investigation, I have a burning need to ensure nothing comes back on them.

With nothing else to do about it right now, I put Kate and her cousin out of mind.

"Joker, turn on something with base." I yell out.

The women pair off with the men as the music changes to a seductive beat. Normally, I would be right in the mix but thoughts of Kate keep me on the sidelines. That doesn't mean I can't enjoy the show. As the night progresses, Jade disentangles from Rocker and drops down in the chair next to me.

"So, you and the teacher, huh?" she asks.

She has something up her sleeve. Her smirk gives her away.

"Jade." My warning goes unheeded.

She barrels on like she always does. "I like her. I think she'd be good for you. You need some sweet to smooth your hard edges."

Despite the fact her words echo my intrigue, I'm not quite ready to admit it out loud.

"Jade, you know we need an in at the high school if we have any hope of getting intel. That's all there is to it." Maybe if I keep throwing out the denial it'll stick.

"Keep lying to yourself, my friend. I'm happy to have a front row seat to the fireworks to come." Her reassuring squeeze to my hand is a contradiction to her no-bullshit response.

Laughing, I pull my hand away and take a drink of my beer as we sit in companionable silence.

This is exactly the life I wanted when I joined the Broken Souls. Living my best life, following our own set of rules, commitment to no one but my MC family. I couldn't ask for anything better.

But then an uncontrollable thought breaks through.

It could be better with a certain wild haired brunette in your lap.

* * *

I approach the unassuming family home of the dead high schooler. Marc and Jean Baker were high school sweethearts. Married at eighteen, they moved into this house the day after their honeymoon. The house is well cared for. It's clear the family takes pride in their modest home. It's reminiscent of the house I grew up in.

While it's not the best time to pay them a visit, it's important to get information as quickly as possible. I hate to disturb them at such a devastating time. If time wasn't working against us, we'd figure out how to get the intel another way.

The door opens as I clear the top step, Kate stopping short when she catches sight of me. "Mac, what are you doing here?"

It's been a few days since I last saw her in that sinful bikini. Three to be exact. Not like I've been counting or anything.

This woman consumes my thoughts, has since the day she ran her shopping cart right into me. I've lost count of the number of times she's invaded my dreams. Wet dreams waking me in the middle of the night ready to blow like a teenager. It takes effort to pull myself from those thoughts. Now is most certainly not the time. "The same as you most likely. Came to pay my respects and offer any help the club can to the family."

I waver in telling her about the club's investigation. Not because I don't trust her but because I don't want to involve her in what we're doing.

While the club members' history and connections aren't common knowledge, that's not a concern I have with her. Limiting knowledge of the club's investigation may be a necessary evil but I don't want to lie to her.

Keeping to ourselves wasn't only for the townspeople's benefit when the club moved here. We intentionally kept our distance to keep people from looking too closely at our extracurricular activities. Some of the brothers still report to Uncle Sam under cover of darkness.

There's also guilt on my conscience, that in a roundabout way, I am using her interest in me to get closer for the club's investigation.

"That's really nice of you and the club. I'm sure they'll appreciate that." Her face softens, a beautiful light shining through her eyes. "Do you want me to introduce you?"

"I'd appreciate it." I'll use any excuse to stay in her presence longer.

And not just for the investigation. There's just something about Kate that intrigues me. This is new territory for me and not one I'm completely comfortable with.

Other than a high school girlfriend my senior year, I've never had a serious relationship. And she knew the relationship was going to end after graduation. I never made a secret of my plan to join the Navy.

My interest in Kate throws me off my game.

Distracted by the sway of her hips, I follow her into the house until a couple sitting close at the kitchen table comes into view. They're huddled together as if to keep each other from falling apart. The man holds her close while the woman quietly sobs on his shoulder.

"Marc, Jean, this is Mac. He's with the Broken Souls Motorcycle Club. They moved to town about six months ago." The husband looks up at Kate's voice.

"Your club is the reason our son is dead! This town didn't have a drug problem until you people moved here." He makes no effort to hide his hatred.

It isn't completely surprising. We've dealt with this kind of hatred and worse over the years.

"Marc! I told you we don't know that for sure." Jean finally lifts her head from her husband's shoulder.

"Sir, I came to pay our respects and offer anything your family might need. Please believe we have nothing to do with any drugs or dealers here or anywhere else." I understand the man's anger.

His grief drives his need to blame someone for his son's death. He's lashing out at the easy target.

"Do you have any idea where your son may have gotten the drugs?" I press gently.

His shoulders slump in defeat. "No, we have no clue. I assumed it was your club when the overdoses started right after you all moved here."

"Sir, I can understand that assumption. A lot of MC's deal drugs and a lot worse, but that's not the Broken Souls."

I make a quick decision to share the truth of our move with them. Hopefully honesty will get past their preconceived notions. "We picked this town because we wanted to make a difference in the community and thought we had a lot to offer here. Being here for the last few months, we still feel that way."

"Like I said, we don't know anything. Jonny was an honor student and had been accepted to Clemson on a full ride scholarship. Jean and I are so proud of him." He breaks off when Jean releases a loud sob, soothing her with his hand on her back.

"If you don't mind, I'll leave my number with you. Reach out if you think of anything that might help." I hold out my hand to shake his after handing him my number.

Heading out the door, I don't realize Kate follows until I hear her voice at my back. "Do you really think you guys can find whoever is dealing drugs?"

"That's what we're trying to do. Believe me, we hate drugs and dealers more than anything. We'll do whatever it takes to bring peace to the families that have lost loved ones." Conviction rings in my voice.

"It's a scary time with these deaths. Aside from some petty crimes, this town hasn't dealt with much of a criminal element." The sadness in her words is a dead giveaway to how affected she is by the teen's death.

It's obviously a pain she hasn't dealt with before. I could tell her it never gets easier. No matter if it's the first person you ever lose or the last, the loss is going to hit you hard. But I keep that to myself. She's dealing with enough.

"Did you know him?" This is the reason I've involved her.

Shitty as I feel to question her, I need to know what she knows.

That flimsy justification doesn't stop the guilt boiling in my gut.

I shove that shit down. This is about keeping any more people from dying.

Keep justifying your actions, asshole.

"He was in my math class. I spent some extra time tutoring him last year so he could keep his eligibility for the team." She chokes back her tears.

"That's right. I remember you work at the high school. You haven't heard any rumors about kids looking to get hooked up for some fun?" Her searching gaze tells me I might be pushing a little too hard.

Joker isn't the only brother that never learned when to quit when he was ahead. "No, I wish there was something I could do to help. I'm heartbroken for what this family has lost." She's on the verge of tears again. That shitty feeling grows when my questions are causing her pain.

I fight the pull I feel for this woman. Resisting the urge to reach out and wrap her up in a hug takes a herculean effort. My arms ache with the need to pull her close, my body yearning for the first feel of her softness fitting to my hardness like pieces of a puzzle.

"How about we exchange numbers? That way we can get in touch if something comes up." This is the perfect excuse to get her number. I want it and not just for the investigation.

I tried lying to myself but in my gut, I know I want to get closer to this woman. Want to get to know her. Figure out what draws me in like a moth to a flame.

"I guess, if you think that will help." She fishes her phone out of her purse before handing it to me.

Expecting some kind of security, I'm surprised to see she doesn't have any kind of a lock when the screen turns on. "You should set up facial recognition or at least a passcode. Anyone could get into your phone with no security like this."

"No one will benefit from getting into my phone. I don't have anything important on it." She waves off my concern like a pesky fly.

I disagree but now isn't the time to get into an argument. Instead, a noncommittal noise is enough to convey my displeasure.

Tapping in my number then calling myself, I wait to hear my ringtone before I hand her phone back. "I know now's not the appropriate time but I was serious about that date. I'd really like to take you out."

I get the same disbelieving look as the last time I asked. I don't understand why she's so shocked.

She's a gorgeous woman with a banging body. Add in the innocence you won't find in my lifestyle.

I want to explore both to solve the puzzle of my interest in her.

I know myself. I'm not the settling down type. No woman has held my interest long enough to change my mind.

At thirty years old, I'm not looking for that yet but there's just something about Kate. It's impossible to get her out of my head.

Believe me, I've tried.

"I'll think about it." Her uncertainty still won't let her give in. "And I'll let you know if I hear anything."

"Be careful. Whoever is selling drugs isn't going to want to be identified now that bodies are dropping." The thought of something happening to her chills me down to my bones.

"Don't worry. I can handle myself. I've been the only one doing it most of my life." Her words reveal more than she intends to. Her obvious feelings of unworthiness hit me right in the gut. I know those feelings well and would do just about anything to take them away from her.

I'm a willing captive to the sway of her hips once again as I sit on my bike, not even hiding the fact I'm enjoying the show she unconsciously puts on.

She doesn't know it but her continued refusal only increases my determination. Makes me want her that much more. Want to bring her into my world and dirty up her pristine exterior.

She might not know it yet but she will soon.

Chapter Six

Kate

This day can't end fast enough.

The thought runs on repeat as I finally cross the threshold at home, grateful to survive another day. I never thought this day would end. It's getting harder as each school year passes to find the motivation to continue on this path.

The chime of my phone shakes me out of my melancholy as I drop my keys and shoes in the entryway.

Mac: Hey gorgeous

Nerves flutter in my belly at the sight of his name on my screen. I have no idea what to say, completely dumbfounded that he actually reached out. Maybe texting will be easier than face-to-face conversation.

God knows, you're not doing so well in person.

Me: Hey Mac. What's up?

Nope, text isn't much better. Could you sound any more lame?

Figuring my ridiculously non-existent conversational skills lost his interest, I set my phone down in the kitchen and grab a bottle of wine.

It's one of my only indulgences and the one thing I've been looking forward to all day. Anticipation of the relaxing night ahead was the only thing that got me through this day.

Glass ready on the counter, my phone chimes again, distracting me from uncorking the bottle.

Just like that, the sight of Mac's name sends the bottle fumbling in my hands.

Shoot can't be spilling the precious alcohol.

Setting the bottle aside to avoid a potential catastrophe, I take a deep breath before picking up my phone.

Uncontrollable butterflies take flight in my belly once again.

Stop it, Kate. You're not a teenager talking to her first crush. Get it together!

Mac: I was thinking about you. Do you have plans tonight?

Mac: I still want that date.

I don't know him well but there is one thing I can say, Mac is relentless when he wants something. I just don't understand what he possibly sees in me.

Okay, so I know I'm not ugly. I'm in decent shape. The healthier life choices can be thanked for that. But I still don't compare to the women I've seen those men with.

And it's not only on the outside. I'm never going to be the sexually carefree, outgoing woman I envision holds his attention.

Sipping my wine, I lean on the counter considering what to say. The man is incredibly sexy, the sheer perseverance of his pursuit a definite boost to my confidence.

Another chime tells me he's beat me to it as *another* text comes through while I'm lost in thought.

He sure is relentless.

Mac: Come on gorgeous. Take a ride with me. I promise if at any time you're uncomfortable I'll take you home. What do you have to lose?

He's right, what do I have to lose?

It's not like there's anything exciting going on at home. With a longing look at my glass of wine, I throw caution to the wind.

Me: Ok, I give up. What time will you pick me up?

Mac: Be there in 30. Put on some jeans and boots

I walk to my bedroom, shaking my head at my dorky thumbs up reply. Unable to resist, I take another sip of my wine as I consider my closet.

Let's see if I have anything appropriate for a ride on a motorcycle.

My favorite skinny jeans should work but my shoe selection is more of a challenge. With my limited social calendar, it's not like I have a need for much variety. I'm limited to dress flats for work and running shoes for everything else. That's about it.

But I'm not giving up.

An eternity later, blowing hair out of my face, I spy a pair of boots in the very recesses of my closet. Doing an army crawl out of the depths of darkness, the doorbell rings right as I'm pulling them on.

Shoot, time got away from me.

But a glance at the clock shows Mac is a few minutes early.

The butterflies are back as I make my way to the door. I stop to press a hand to my belly in an attempt to calm them.

I take a deep breath for courage, pausing with my hand on the door handle until I think I have myself under control.

After a quick pep talk, I pull the door open. Only for the air to rush right back out when my eyes land on Mac.

I'm kidding myself. I have no hope of steeling my nerves against this man.

He's the picture of hot sexy bad boy, arms crossed as he leans against the door frame. One ankle crossed over the other, worn denim molds to strong thighs. Under his jacket, his t-shirt stretches tight across the firm muscles of his chest before falling loose around his stomach.

There must be classes – 10 steps to get women to drop their panties.

Giggling internally, my perusal continues without conscious thought.

His hair is sexily mused. He obviously rode here on his motorcycle.

His eyes snare mine when I finally reach his face, distracting me from the vision of him on the cover of a steamy romance novel. His sexy grin, dimples on display, muscles bulging under his jacket. He'd be the perfect model.

His eyes take a journey of their own over my body. My skin tingles as though he mapped my curves with his hands. The appreciation in his gaze impossible to miss when his eyes finally connect with mine. My panties are soaked from that one look.

"Hey gorgeous. You look beautiful."

It takes effort, but I break our hypnotizing connection to look down at myself.

"I hope this is okay. I assumed we would be on your motorcycle. I've never been on one before, so I wasn't sure what to wear."

He takes my question as an open invitation to run his hot gaze over my body once more. This time even slower.

Don't hyperventilate. You don't need to be fainting in front of this gorgeous man.

Although mouth-to-mouth may not be a bad idea.

"You're perfect." Shivers skate down my spine, a throbbing pulse ending in my core.

This man could read me a grocery list and that smooth voice would still turn me on.

I watch as he reaches up to wrap a wayward curl around his finger. All the while his mesmerizing eyes continue to hypnotize me.

I'm powerless to the draw to him. I somehow stop my forward momentum, really hoping he doesn't notice the fool I was about to make of myself. If he did, he's gentleman enough not to call me on it.

"Do you have a leather jacket? I don't want you to get cold. I thought we could take that ride through the mountains you recommended."

I can't believe he remembers that from our earlier conversation. Such a sexy contradiction of cocky bad boy with a surprisingly nice guy hidden beneath. So different than I expected, he's done nothing but keep me on my toes since I barreled into him in the grocery store.

"I think so. Let me look." I find one in the very back of the closet, I pull it on while following Mac out to his motorcycle.

The huge matte black machine is intimidating. The illumination from the street light throwing it half in light, half in shadow, makes it look even more sinister.

He has to be strong to control that big machine. It's no wonder his muscles are so defined.

My pulse skyrockets when I realize how up close and personal our bodies are about to be.

Unaware of my lustful thoughts, he sets a black helmet on my head. His fingers brush my skin as he works efficiently to strap it securely under my chin like it's no big deal.

I'm riveted by the easy way he swings his leg over the machine after securing his own helmet. The play of the light highlights Mac sitting confidently astride his motorcycle. He's an extension of the machine. Like he's done this for years.

My mind blanks. My mouth turns to dust. My panties soak.

Everything about this man gets me hot.

Then I notice there's not much room behind him on the seat. His large body takes up most of the available space and I'm about to be squeezed on there with him. Mistaking my hesitation, he raises a helping hand to help me on the motorcycle.

Cue the hyperventilating.

Studying the machine like it's a puzzle I need to solve, I'm relieved at the assistance from Mac.

I have no idea what I'm doing.

A shock of electricity passes between us when our hands touch for the first time.

Oh wow. If just an innocent touch of our hands is that electric – what kind of fireworks will I see when his hands touch other parts of my body?

A squeeze to my hand brings me back to my current dilemma. "I got you."

I take a deep breath and try to emulate the smooth swing of his leg over the machine.

My short legs hinder my mobility so trying to swing a leg over the seat takes a tremendous amount of effort that sends the machine rocking. No gracefulness in my movements, I'm as awkward as I worried I would be climbing on behind him.

And that was a complete failure.

Thank God he isn't looking back to see my cheek's heating. I settle on the machine with an inch of space between our bodies.

His effortless grace sure was deceptive.

I watch in confusion as he leans down to drop pegs from each side of the motorcycle.

"Set your feet here." His deep rumbling order has my feet moving automatically, lifting one leg then the other to rest on them.

And then I sit here with no idea what to do next. Mac takes the decision out of my hands before I have to figure it out. Reaching back, his hand on my lower back pulls me flush against him. Effectively eliminating the distance between my core and his backside.

Oh. Do we need to be this close?

And he's not done. Taking both my hands he uses his hold to pull me flush to his back. "Wrap your arms around my waist." Voice like gravel, his growled words sent my mind spinning.

How on Earth am I going to survive this ride without self-combusting?

The leather of his vest is a hot brand tightening my nipples where I'm pressed to his back from my breasts to my core. His body heat obviously warming the supple material.

Even more wetness escapes to soak my panties. Pretty sure they're ruined at this point.

Lost in my internal struggle, my hands instinctively tighten where I clutch his stomach when the beast roars beneath us, almost positive he felt it too. If the clench of the muscles under my hands is any indication.

The rumbling beast between my thighs does nothing to calm my arousal.

"Hang on." That's the only warning I get before he backs out of my driveway. Revving the engine, he drives slowly down the otherwise quiet street.

Nerves that had calmed at the slow speed furiously return as he accelerates onto Main Street.

Those nerves momentarily overpower my arousal. I try to burrow my head between his shoulder blades. Unfortunately, the helmet on my head doesn't allow me to hide my face much.

The machine between my legs rumbles louder as we pick up speed.

I finally grow enough courage to lift my head for a peek over his shoulder. The stunning scenery passing by mesmerizes me as we ride down the open road. The beauty of the passing landscape captures my rapt attention.

It's a beautiful experience that will live in my memory for the rest of my life.

Mac handles the bike with a quiet confidence that calms my nerves.

Loosening my death grip on his waist, I flatten my hands over the hard planes of his abs. His muscles contract under my hands again. He drops a hand from the handlebars to press my palms tighter to his muscles.

With my arms wrapped around his strong body, I get lost in the beauty around us as we take a winding path up into the surrounding mountains. Disappointment fills me when the motorcycle rolls to a stop at a spot high up in the mountains.

Wow. That went faster than I thought it would.

We gaze out at the scene in front of us in the deafening silence when he cuts the engine.

There's a peacefulness in the sudden quiet. The breathtaking view of the valley eclipsed only by the sight of Mac glancing over his shoulder.

A sinful grin graces his face as he removes his helmet and twists around, the masculine move drool worthy. "How was it?"

"I loved it!" I could no more hide the wide grin stretching my face than the excitement ringing in my voice.

Never have I felt such freedom in my life.

Growing up with my controlling father, I never had the opportunity to try anything he considered too dangerous. It was a *long* list of things not to do.

"Why did we stop?" Not that I'm complaining but I am curious.

"I figured you'd enjoy watching the sunset over the mountains before we head back to town."

Smile still gracing my face, it grows impossibly bigger at his words. "That sounds just about perfect."

"Have you ever come up here to see it?" He asks.

"No, I've never been here." My smile dims with my embarrassment. Still, I don't say what I really mean.

I never took the risk.

"Then you're in for a treat." He promises as his helping hand extends to help me off the motorcycle. I shouldn't be surprised when another shock runs up my arm at the contact.

But I am.

I'd like to say I swung myself off the bike with grace. Sadly, the only amazing thing about my move is I don't fall flat on my face when my feet hit the ground. The unsteadiness in my legs catches me completely off guard. Not expecting the jelly-ness, my free hand unconsciously latches onto the hard muscle of Mac's shoulder.

Don't need to embarrass myself by collapsing.

His muscles flex under my hand. And, of course, his smooth dismount is much more graceful than mine. Something I could never hope to emulate.

The sexy display sets my heart racing again. Officially reigniting my desire. Everything this man does sets me on fire.

Thankfully, he keeps any comments about my awkwardness to himself as he reaches up to quickly remove our helmets.

"Come here." Not really giving me a choice, he settles his backside sideways against his motorcycle.

Another sexy position he probably learned in that 10 step course.

Unaware of my inner voice, he uses his hold on my hand to pull me into the open space between his legs. The heat of his chest presses hard to my back, his arms wrap tight around my waist, enveloping me in his heat. My butt settles right into his lap. I've never felt this level of protection and contentment in my life. And let's not forget arousing.

It's like coming home. Like I've always belonged here.

No matter how routine, his every move lights a fire inside me. I can't stop the shiver the runs up and down my entire body.

"Cold?" His question is accompanied by his hands roaming up and down my sides, the upward motion brings them intoxicatingly close to my breasts. My flesh swells at the mental image of him continuing up to cup them.

"Just a little." It takes everything I have to mask my body's response, barely holding back a whimper when he hugs me close to the heat of his body. He's like a furnace. Burning straight to the heart of me.

"I'll keep you warm." His hot breath coasts over the sensitive skin of my neck. His arms tighten like a band around my waist, pulling me impossibly closer.

A whimper catches in the back of my throat. My brain turns to mush. All I can do is *feel.*

I'm caught up in the sensations. The mix of his cologne, combined with the unique scent that is all Mac, an aphrodisiac. His body surrounding me, the hardness pressing against my butt impossible to miss.

I hold still in his arms. Waiting with bated breath for his next move.

The anticipation is agonizing.

What feels like an eternity later, one of his hands takes a leisurely path from my waist up to my neck. The move leaves a trail of goosebumps in his wake.

With a featherlike touch, the rough pads of his fingers are a fire branding my skin as he brushes my curls aside to expose the column of my neck. A shudder exhales out of me at the contact.

I never knew how sensitive my skin is there.

Burying his face in that same spot, his lips are an erotic brush lighting sparks over my skin. My body is aflame. I feel him in every pore. Every place we touch is a live wire set to explode.

"You smell so good. Wonder what you taste like right here." The wet heat of his tongue slowly licks over the spot he just inhaled.

Shivers wrack my body from the heat of his mouth. My skin overheats at his suction on the tender flesh. Explosions detonate across my sensitive skin as his tongue strokes over the erogenous zone.

The moans escaping my mouth are impossible to control. I tilt my head unconsciously to give him more access. My hips shift without permission, my butt rubbing wantonly against his hardness. A groan rumbles from his chest through my back at my movement, finishing in a rush over my skin. Wetness escapes my core at the competing sensations.

The power of the arousal flowing through me is scary. Never has my body had such a visceral reaction to a man. And he hasn't even kissed me.

I might not be a virgin but the man behind me is so far beyond my limited experience it's laughable.

Mac's movements show none of the doubts I struggle with daily. He's a man who knows exactly who he is, what he wants.

The hand in my hair travels to my neck in teasing strokes, lightning shooting straight to my clit. Tender fingers glide along my jaw, turning my face to his.

His electric blue eyes snare mine as Mac lifts his face to look down at me. Breath heaves from my lungs as I eagerly anticipate his next move.

"Just a little taste."

Locked in his hypnotic stare, heat pooling in my core, running down to coat my inner thighs, I can do nothing but nod.

I'm not even sure what I'm agreeing to.

I just know I need more.

More of him. More of these sensations. More of the feelings he invokes inside me.

It's all the permission he needs to swoop in. His mouth takes complete control of mine. Teasing me with sharp bites before sucking my lower lip into his mouth, the sharp bite of his teeth just enough pressure to force a gasp from my lips.

The beauty around us fades away as he sweeps me up in a sexual awakening.

It's a feast for my senses as the chemistry between us lights up my entire body.

The fire in my veins boiling my blood. It burns me from the inside out.

But he's not done. No, he continues his assault on my senses. Building my desire to peaks I've never known.

Taking advantage of the gasp parting my lips, his tongue invades my mouth. It's a leisurely exploration as he learns the shape of my mouth.

His skillful strokes teasingly tempt my tongue to play. A shiver ripples down my spine. Any hesitation I had flees as my tongue dances with his.

Another groan rumbles through my back as he deepens the kiss. I swear his sole purpose to drive me mad. No longer teasing, his mastery drives my pursuit, falling into his trap as he sucks my tongue into his own mouth.

His firm hold on my jaw anchors me to him, holding me exactly where he wants for his sensual manipulations. It's all I can do to reach my hand up, fingers grasping his hair to hold on for the ride.

My breasts rub erotically inside the lace of my bra as I lift my arms. It only serves to add another layer of arousal to my already overheated body.

I'm lost in the desire he stokes in me. Never have I felt this level of arousal rising up like a tidal wave. A razor's edge between pain and euphoria, bringing with it newfound feelings of freedom and confidence.

Chapter Seven

Mac

A trembling Kate in my arms is an aphrodisiac as I continue building her desire. Her body melts against mine like her life goal is to burrow deep down into my soul.

Her responsiveness doesn't surprise me.

Her innocence is misleading. There's no way to hide the passion beneath the surface. She just hasn't had an opportunity to explore her sensuality yet. My adrenaline spikes, just imagining her sexual awakening.

And if I have any say, I'll be the man lucky enough to guide her exploration.

She's a siren in my arms. Luring my desire to out of control levels. My mind spins, imagining all the ways I want to take her.

Regretfully, I slow the kiss, decreasing the pressure of my mouth while I still have some working brain cells left.

I could spend hours, days, just kissing her. Exploring the depths of her mouth. Watching the flush rise in her cheeks. Imagining how far down that gorgeous body it goes. If I play my cards right, it'll be worth the wait. That promise to myself gives me the strength to pull back.

I savor the moment before I push her too far too soon, unable to resist one last taste as my tongue follows her retreat. Her fingers threading through my hair are a test of my restraint, gripping the strands to pull me back to her.

I somehow find the will to disengage. Moving to rest my forehead on hers, I marvel at the beauty in front of me.

There's no way to hide the truth of the words pouring from my mouth. "As sweet as I thought you'd be." My whisper fans across her cheek as I trail my mouth up to her ear.

Eyes fluttering open, the picture of her flushed face will be burned in my memory for eternity. The vision in front of me reused over and over again with my hand around my dick.

I've had more women than I can count but the raw desire Kate has no hope of hiding will be a sight I will never forget.

Sliding my other hand from her jaw to a safer place on her waist, I hug her against me once more. My fingers rub soothing circles on her stomach. I hold her tight as we both turn our gazes to the horizon, catching the last hues of pink fading from the sunset we almost missed – too caught up in each other.

The feel of her wrapped in my arms, as close as we can be, is intoxicating. It's perfection. More right than anything I've ever experienced in my life.

As the sun fully drops behind the mountain, the tension in Kate's body tightens with each second of light that disappears.

It doesn't take a genius to recognize she's chastising herself for her wanton behavior.

"I've been all over the world and can honestly say this is one of the most beautiful sunsets I've ever seen." I speak candidly, my only goal to get her out of her head, realizing too late I'm sharing a part of myself I hadn't intended.

"Really?" The surprised look she throws over her shoulder is full of questions but that's all she says.

Too late to take it back, I inhale a deep breath to share a part of myself I haven't shared with any other woman. I have to be willing to open myself up if I want her to do the same.

"Yeah, it's the combination of peacefulness and tranquility. I've always loved the mountains. Being in the Navy for so long, I didn't get much of this."

"Do you miss it?" She asks.

"Yes and no. Sometimes I miss exploring new places. But what was most important to me, making a difference and the team camaraderie, I get that with the MC. I served with most of my brothers, so it's not much different now. It just comes in a different package."

"I don't know what that's like. Having close friends. My father didn't encourage that." Her offhand comment saddens me.

That sadness is quickly overcome with anger. Parents are supposed to be their kids' biggest supporters. He clearly failed her. What I wouldn't give to have that asshole in front of me.

She turns back to the view with a pensive look, her subject change directed to the open air. "I've lived here my entire life and never experienced this beauty in all that time."

I debate how to respond. Ultimately, going with vagueness to avoid overwhelming her. "Maybe it's time to broaden your horizons."

I don't know when my feelings started changing but it becomes my mission to get her out of her shell. I want to encourage her to try new things. Without scaring her away.

She seems to catch my double meaning. "I think you're right."

Her next question comes out of left field. "Have you found anything new about the drug dealing?"

I stiffen against her. Everything in me screams to keep her as far from the investigation as I possibly can. Even though I know it's probably the fastest way to get answers, I worry that I won't be able to protect her if she shakes the wrong tree on her own.

I give her a half truth. "We're still looking for a connection at the school. So far, nothing has popped up."

Giving her one last hard squeeze, I regretfully drop my arms. My conscious screaming that it's best to end the night before it gets any later. "We should probably head back."

The disappointment on her face gives me hope she isn't second guessing our kiss. "You're right. I'm not usually out this late on a school night."

Hands on her hips, because I just can't stop myself, I gently move her away so I can turn back to my bike. I quickly strap her helmet on then help her on the bike. She's a perfect fit behind me. Her legs spread to accommodate my body between them. The heat of her pussy burns where it presses tight to my ass.

Procrastinating as long as possible, I stick to a slower pace back down the mountain, not ready for our night to end just yet.

The longer we ride, the more I wrestle with the rightness in my soul at the feel of her at my back.

When we come to a stop in her driveway, I once again reach back to help her off the bike, her easy acceptance a testament to the trust she's starting to place in me.

A frown crosses my face as I climb off the bike, not happy with the sight of her darkened porch as I walk her up the steps. "You should have a light on out here at night. It's not safe for a single woman alone in the darkness."

My overprotectiveness is already rearing its head.

"You're right. It's usually on but I keep forgetting to replace the bulb. It burned out last week." Her sheepish expression raises my protective instincts even higher.

I'll have to get that taken care of.

"Will you come to the clubhouse with me this weekend? We're having a party on Saturday and I'd love for you to be there." And I really mean it.

I want her to come and not just because of the investigation. Or the thought of fucking her.

This is new territory for me. My strong reaction to her scares me. I don't know if I'm ready for more but I just can't seem to help myself.

I don't want our time together to end yet. And I fear it will all too soon. I have an inexplicable need to see where our connection goes.

"I don't know. I don't think I'll fit in." Her self-doubt hard to miss, hesitancy comes through loud and clear both on her face and in her voice.

"You won't." I quickly realize my mistake when hurt crosses her face from my careless words.

Unable to resist touching her, I cup her cheek while quickly correcting my screw up. "I mean that in a good way. I meant you won't fit in because the other women just can't hold a candle to you. There's something refreshing about you."

I see the reassurance works, her face lights up and she leans in to my touch. The softness of her delicate skin impossible to ignore so I don't, instead running my fingertips back and forth over there flushed cheek.

Relief rolls through me at her easy acceptance and tilt of her head to press her cheek closer to my palm.

"I'm still not sure. Can I let you know by Friday?"

Caressing my fingertips along her cheek, I get lost in the softness I fear I'll never get enough of. "Sure, text me when you decide."

I need to give her a heads up about the parties. I don't want what she might see there to set back the progress I've made. "The parties can get wild. I don't want to scare you away but I also don't want you walking in blind. There's probably going to be some things you're not used to seeing. Just know, if at any point you get uncomfortable, all you need to do is tell me. I'll be right there beside you."

A nod is the best answer I'm gonna get tonight.

I can't resist leaning in to press a gentle kiss to her forehead before moving down the porch steps.

"I'll wait for you to get inside and lock the door. Goodnight Kate." My feet echo the regret in my voice at the night ending.

"Goodnight Mac." She unlocks and opens the door, quietly closing herself inside.

I wait for the sound of the lock engaging before returning to my bike for the short ride back to the clubhouse. I have a feeling she'll be ruling my dreams long after I fall asleep.

Chapter Eight

Kate

Spending the weekend cleaning the house top to bottom leaves me with a feeling of accomplishment I carry into Monday morning when I wake early for my morning run. With that necessary but evil torture out of the way, I dress for the day on an endorphin high.

I'm ready for a new week.

As I walk down Main Street, I'm mentally planning my schedule for the return of students this week.

While the journey is routine, I take everything in with new eyes. A new lightness in my step, a fresh perspective.

The police station sits on the corner of the block. It and the church are some of the oldest buildings in Frostown. That age is reflected in the old brick exterior. While worn, both buildings have withstood the test of time.

The diner directly across the street has been a staple in town for as long as I can remember. Always busy, no matter the time of day or day of the week, you'll always find the place packed. It's also most likely where you'll find all the busy bodies gathered, getting up in everyone's business.

Gotta love small town living.

Dean's Bar is between the diner and the new bakery. Dean caters to sports fans with several large screen televisions, pool tables, dart boards and even a small dance floor. He recently started offering Friday night karaoke specials and live bands once a month.

He's given the locals a place to hang out rather than taking the longer trips to the bigger cities for entertainment. More importantly, he's keeping their money local, the revenue reinvested in our community.

More small businesses line the rest of the historic street, including the new bakery that opened a few months ago. I've done my best to avoid the temptation but just can't resist today.

Buoyed with a wave of confidence, I walk through the door of Sweet Treats. The old-fashioned bell rings out to announce my presence, the scent of yummy temptation luring me in further.

Trying not to be too obvious in my curiosity, I check out the interior with interest, impressed with the vibe of the bakery.

Bright white walls showcase a colorfully eclectic décor.

Wonder if the look of the place matches the owner's personality.

The chrome tables complimented by black framed chairs with teal upholstery. The black and white checkered floor so shiny I can almost see my reflection. The whole place has 1950's rockabilly vibe. It's a refreshing contrast to the down-home feel of the surrounding businesses.

Maybe this is just what our small town needs.

At the same time the thought crosses my mind, a voice calls out from the back. "Be right with you!"

I can't place the accent in those words but it's definitely not from around here. I guess the rumors are true, an outsider moved to town and set up shop. My curiosity grows beyond the delightful goodies on display at the counter.

Even a loner like me has heard the gossip and rumors. Some people in town are uncomfortable with the new arrival, fearful of upsetting the dynamic of their small town. It's no surprise the townsfolk are set in their ways.

Adapting to change is *so* not this town's motto.

What would entice an out of towner to set up shop in our small town?

Even though there's no sign of the body belonging to the voice, my manners prompt a response, rudeness unacceptable. "No need to rush. I'm just checking things out."

Minutes later, a curvy blond hurries in from the back where I assume she was elbow deep creating more magical goodies. At least, I hope they're magical, the ones on display look to die for.

She stands behind the counter drying her hands, all while gifting me a friendly smile. "Sorry about that. What can I do for you?"

"Everything looks so good, I can't decide. Any recommendations?" I ask.

"As you can see from these hips, I love it all." Her laughter is loud and boisterous. "Seriously though, it depends on your preferences. If you like a little sin in your breakfast, the chocolate croissant is to die for. The blueberry muffins are a classic with a streusel topping. And of course, you can never go wrong with any of the other muffins."

Drool pools in my mouth. Each delicious description tempting but I don't even have to think about what I want.

Chocolate always wins with me. "I'll take the chocolate croissant."

"My kind of girl. You won't regret it." Her early morning cheer is contagious.

Even better, her personality is a soulmate to my inner voice.

She rocks a uniform in line with the rockabilly vibe. Her curves fill out the outfit perfectly. There's no way I could ever hope to pull that off.

I'd look like a Halloween contest reject.

I offer my hand after she sets my indulgent breakfast in a pink box. Intentionally pushing myself out of my comfort zone, I return her friendly smile. "I'm Kate. I haven't been in here yet but I hear great things from the other teachers."

This is definitely not my norm but I have a good feeling about her.

Nothing ventured, nothing gained.

"Nice to meet you. I'm Demi. Now that we know each other, you'll have to give me your honest opinion on the croissant." A wink accompanies her smile. She says it jokingly but I have a feeling she's serious.

"Of course." I say with my own conspiratorial grin.

"So, you work at a school, is it the high school down the block?" She asks.

"Yes, I'm a math teacher there." I tell her, waiting for the inevitable groan when people learn which subject I teach.

She doesn't disappoint. "Oh god! I hate math! I don't think we can be friends," she teases.

Surprising myself, I don't even hesitate to throw it right back her way. "Don't worry. I promise I won't test you."

"Please don't. So, did you grow up here? Most of the people I've met have lived here their entire lives." She seems genuinely interested.

"I did." I answer. "I live in the same house I grew up in a block over from here. I went away for college but came back after graduation. I couldn't imagine settling down anywhere else."

"I can see why. I've only been here a few months and it's the perfect hidden gem. What I've seen of it anyway. I've been pretty busy getting the bakery up and running so I can't completely agree with you yet." She teases as she hands me the croissant. "Do you want a coffee to go with that croissant?"

"Sure, I'll take an iced mocha."

"Ahh, one of my specialties." She turns to make my coffee but catches my not so subtle move as I lift the box to sniff my treat. "It tastes even better than it smells."

So much for trying to be discreet in my gluttony.

It's obvious she's amused but at least she's not laughing in my face.

The blush creeping up my face is a sign I may have taken too big a leap out of my comfort zone. "I'm sure it will. I can't wait to try it."

"Remember you promised to give me your honest opinion on it."

The mouthwatering smell almost distracts me from the time before I realize I need to get moving. I swear angels sing when I take a quick sip of the irresistible caffeine. "Oh wow. This is great."

If the coffee is this good, I can't even imagine what the croissant will do to me.

"The coffee is good, but my pastries are to die for." It almost sounds like a warning.

I haven't laughed this much in years. With a promise to stop back in after school I head out the door to get my day started.

Despite my sniffing blunder, I'm proud of myself for the new experience.

Maybe this friend thing isn't as impossible as I thought it would be.

***

The day passes in a blur. Before I know it, I'm walking out the gates of the school on my way home, my sense of accomplishment still going strong from this morning.

The start of the school year is always a struggle to pivot from the fun of summer to the focus of schoolwork. I'm right there with my students in the struggle.

Looking forward to my promise to stop back in the bakery, my feet float down Main Street to the bakery. The tinkling of the bell announces my return.

Demi stands sentry behind the counter, boxing up the few leftover pastries that must not have sold today.

"Hey Kate! Have a good day?" Her exuberant greeting bounces off the walls, loud even though we're the only two people in the bakery.

"Hi Demi." My greeting much quieter. "Yes, I did. I think I'm on my way to wrangling the kids back into the swing of the school year."

"Oh God, I don't miss those days."

Demi's boisterous personality sneaks through to my inner self.

"Yes! I don't know what I was thinking when I decided to become a teacher. I love the summers but go through the same struggles as the students every August." I surprise myself with my openness.

"What made you decide to become a teacher?" She asks.

"My father was the principal at the high school. He expected me to follow in his footsteps and he wasn't one to take no for an answer." She studies me as I finish my explanation.

I'm embarrassed that I've shared something so personal with a virtual stranger but her friendliness just makes it so easy to talk to her. She doesn't seem to take herself too seriously, makes me comfortable opening up about my internal struggles.

Clearing my throat, I go for a subject change to cover my overshare. "I'm here to deliver on my promise to give you an honest opinion. I think all I need to say is I had to guard that deliciousness with my life this morning. Otherwise, it would have been snatched away when I wasn't looking."

"I told you it was to die for." Her grin is nothing if not cocky.

"It definitely was. If your other pastries are even half as good as that croissant, I may be expanding my wardrobe in more ways than one."

An alert from my phone interrupts our conversation. Pulling it from my purse, I see a text from Mac.

Mac: Hey gorgeous. I hate to do this but I have to cancel this weekend. Something came up and I need to go on a run for the club.

Lost in my disappointment, I almost forget I'm not alone.

"You okay? You look like someone actually did steal your favorite croissant." She reads me easily, recognizing my shift in mood, she adds a wink to lighten my mood.

"Yes. Sorry. I got a message from someone canceling our plans this weekend." I'm not even sure why I'm disappointed.

I spent my days since I saw him going back and forth with my inner voice on the pros and cons of taking him up on his invite. I finally settled on the fact that I wouldn't be comfortable in that environment and decided not to take Mac up on his offer to spend time at his clubhouse.

With that reminder, I don't give myself time to think too hard on my disappointment as I respond to him.

Me: No problem have a safe trip.

"You sure you're okay?" Demi presses. "I know we don't know each other that well but I've been told I'm a great listener. And an even better shoulder to cry on if ya need it."

Other than this morning, I don't remember the last time I laughed this much. Needing to talk to someone about my conflicting emotions, I explain the situation, ending with my confusion about Mac canceling on me when I already decided not to go.

"Girl, you like him and you're worried he's just looking to have some fun." Demi has no problem calling me out on what's truly bothering me.

"You're right. I have no idea what he sees in me." The real truth behind my worry escapes.

"That's a no brainer." Seeing my confusion, she breaks it down for me. "Kate, you're a beautiful woman and you seem to have it all together."

She obviously doesn't know me. There's no way I can compare to the sexy women I've seen with the bikers. I'm not anything special.

"I can see you don't believe me." Still has no problem calling me out. "Look, I know we just met but I can see us becoming friends."

I think she might be right.

She rolls right on, not giving me a chance to respond. "I'm new-ish to town. I think that calls for a girl's night. What do you say? Want to have some fun Friday night?"

Considering how seldom I socialize, I find myself wanting to take the chance. I'm the only one with the power to change my lonely existence.

And that starts with putting myself out there.

"Okay. You convinced me. Let's do it." Her excitement is contagious, for once I make no effort to contain my own.

"Great. I've seen the biker bar outside of town but something tells me we'll have to work our way up to that. We'll have to find somewhere a little less intimidating for our first night out."

Debating the options, slim as they are, we settle on Dean's Bar.

Time flies as we chat like old friends.

Demi moved here from California to start the bakery. While she worked for a small bakery there, it's been her dream to open a shop of her own. The coffee is a staple but her true passion is the baked treats.

I'm surprised to see it's growing dark when I glance out the window. It's a rare day when I spend hours in conversation with anyone besides April.

With a promise to stop by again, I say goodbye to Demi and head home, basking in the glorious sunset as I wander down Main Street.

April is doing homework on the couch when I walk through the door.

I can't resist teasing her. "Homework on the first day? Even I decided not to torture my students like that."

She stands with a slam of her book. "I'm just trying to get a head start on things. The assignment isn't due for another week."

The rest of the night is spent cooking dinner together before I relax with a glass of wine.

By the time I slide under my covers with my raunchy romance, I've almost forgotten my disappointment in Mac blowing me off.

Chapter Nine

Kate

By Friday afternoon, I'm eagerly anticipating my night out with Demi.

I know. It's a surprise to me too.

My students are still overwhelmed with the start of the school year. So that's made all my classes a test of patience this week.

I'm definitely looking forward to the time when we all fall into the familiar routine of the school year where the days don't feel like such a challenge.

I hurry through the gates of the school on my way to Sweet Treats. Ready to finalize plans with Demi for tonight. Color me surprised to see the ladies from the club gathered around a table when I walk through the door.

Their laughter rings through the bakery. Wishing I could just let go like that, I send a shy smile their way then hurry over to where Demi stands at the counter, finishing up with another customer.

"Girl, you survived the week! Are you ready for tonight?" Demi's wide grin is infectious as usual.

I've learned during my daily visits to the bakery that Demi isn't afraid to show her emotions.

Or speak her mind.

Not having any other friends in town, she's bulldozing her way past my quiet shell – somehow pulling me out of it.

"I am. Dean's still good?" I ask for the millionth time.

The biker bar is out of the question. No way would I have the courage to walk through those doors. The other day, I had offered the only other options in town, Dean's Bar or the Glass Slipper.

Dean's Bar is conveniently located next door to the bakery where Demi lives in the upstairs apartment. Even though it sits dead center on Main Street, the Friday night crowd still gets a little rowdy.

The other choice is The Glass Slipper, a seedy bar right outside of town that caters to a sketchier clientele. I've never had the nerve to step foot inside but that doesn't mean I haven't heard stories of fights breaking out there most nights.

Have I mentioned how much this town loves gossip?

Demi took pity on me and chose Dean's when I couldn't hide my anxiety over the other bars. I don't trust the type of people we may run into at the Glass Slipper. Just like the biker bar, I'm not quite ready for that experience.

I can't help confirming one more time. "Are you sure you're okay going to Dean's?"

For her first night out, Demi is looking for the excitement you could expect more from the Glass Slipper. "I think we should save The others for another time." Her quick answer makes it clear she already knows me, recognizing I'll be more comfortable at Dean's.

"Hey Kate! Did I hear you ladies are going out tonight?" Jade jumps into our conversation from her perch at the table with the ladies from the club.

Ever the extrovert, Demi beats me to answering. "Yep." She pops the p loudly. "I've convinced Kate she needs some excitement in her life. We're heading to Dean's tonight."

The women chatter excitedly before Jade speaks up again. "You mind if we come with? The men are on a run and we could use a ladies night. Besides Mac would want someone to watch out for Kate."

I tilt my head down, hoping to avoid Demi's probing gaze, hiding my heated cheeks at the mention of Mac's name.

"Is that the guy who blew you off this weekend?" She doesn't let my attempt at avoidance slide.

Jade laughs as she joins us at the counter. "Kate, I've never seen Mac as depressed as he was when he had to cancel with you this weekend. He moped around the clubhouse for hours before the guys left for their run." She says all this with a conspiratory nudge to my shoulder like she didn't just rock my world with her words.

And just like that, the butterflies are back in my belly.

Why does that make me so happy?

I remind myself – yet again – I already decided not to see him again. There's no need to get excited at the idea of him missing me.

"Well, I say it's his loss." Demi boasts. "We're going to get dolled up and have a blast tonight. Kate won't even remember his name by the end of the night."

"I don't think he's going to like that." Jade laughs. "In fact, I'd venture to say he'll do anything in his power to make himself unforgettable."

A bark of laughter escapes me at their craziness but I ignore Jade's prediction to address Demi. "I wouldn't go that far. I think your idea of having a blast is much different than mine."

"We'll see." Demi's devious smile sets off warning bells in my head but she ignores my probing look, dismissing it to answer Jade's earlier question. "The more the merrier, I always say. You girls want to meet us at Kate's or at the bar?"

"We'll meet you at Kate's if that's alright with you?" Jade responds to Demi but she's looking at me.

That gives me pause.

While I've become more comfortable with Demi, I'm not sure if I'm ready for the group of ladies in front of me. Something tells me they may be more than I can handle.

I also have April to think about. I hate to invade the house with a group of ladies she doesn't know. At the same time, it might be good to give her a little push like Demi has with me.

Maybe not quite like Demi. She would bulldoze over me if I let her but a gentle nudge couldn't hurt April.

"Okay, sure we can do that. April will be home. So maybe we can keep the shenanigans to a minimum." I agree with a pointed look at Demi.

"Of course. While she is too young for me to corrupt just yet, you are fair game." Her cackle has me rethinking our night out but I really do want to go.

With plans made – the girls will meet at my house at eight – I head back out the door, rushing home to warn April.

It's not a shock when April locks herself in her room after dinner. Her excuse, a paper to write this weekend. I'm not an idiot. I know the real reason. She isn't quite ready to meet all the ladies.

I give her the out and head to the bathroom to wash away the day, careful not to get my hair wet. There is no way I'll be ready on time if I have to tame my wild curls after a wash.

Throwing on my robe, I'm looking through my closet when the doorbell rings. *Shoot, I lost track of time yet again.*

I rush to the door, checking to make sure it's the ladies before pulling it open.

Demi leads the way as they all spill into my home.

Looks like they brought the party with them.

"You're not ready yet?" Demi states the obvious as I look down at myself.

"Sorry, I was just deciding what to wear."

My cheeks heat as I take them in. All of them wear sexy outfits showing *a lot* of skin. I would never be able to pull off those looks.

Not that they don't look great. They do. But I would be way too self-conscious to dare leave the house dressed like that.

Demi takes charge as usual. "Come on, show me to your room. I'll help you find something sexy."

I tell the girls to help themselves after showing them to the kitchen.

Then I take Demi's hand and drag her down the hallway. "Demi, I don't have anything close to what you're all wearing."

The soft material of my robe soaks up the moisture on my palms as I rub my hands down my hips. It's that or wring them in agitation, worried anything in my closet is going to make me stand out from them.

And not in a good way.

"Don't worry, I actually brought you something." Demi proceeds to pull a dress out of her bag. Getting a closer look at it, I know there's no way I'm going to be comfortable in that scrap of fabric.

I'm already shaking my head.

"I don't know, Demi. It doesn't look like it will fit." I don't want to hurt her feelings, so I don't say what I'm really feeling.

There is no way I'll be comfortable in that.

Her laughter lights another blush on my cheeks.

She's almost as good as Mac at that. Making me blush.

"Girl, trust me. It'll fit and you will look hot. And that there is the entire point of tonight. We're getting you out of your comfort zone and having fun. You'll have *a lot* of fun in this dress. I have makeup too. I'm going to help you get ready."

Knowing when I'm beat, I take the dress to my bathroom to slip it on.

The silky black fabric glides down my body, settling in perfectly to caress my curves.

Taking a deep breath for courage, I return to my bedroom where Demi waits to transform me. "Relax, I'm not doing much. We're going to do a few things to enhance your beautiful eyes. That's all."

Feeling a little better, I sit at my vanity, turning to where she has everything set up.

Fifteen minutes, and a lot of chatter later, she's running a pomade through my hair to tame my curls. Finally, she steps back with a shrill whistle. "Damn girl. If I didn't love dick, I would make the switch for you."

Cheeks on fire, I duck my head and laugh off her compliment before standing to check myself in the floor length mirror behind my door.

This can't be me.

The wide straps of the dress stretch to my shoulders, showcasing a short plunging neckline with just a hint of cleavage. The skirt falls flatteringly over my curves to mid-thigh, the toned muscles I've honed on full display like I've never shown them before.

Demi kept her promise. My makeup is subtle, with only a smoky eye that makes my green eyes pop.

"Wow." I'm unable to hide my shock at the woman in the mirror.

"I know right. I'm a magician." She'd probably pat herself on the back if she could reach. "Now, let's find you some shoes and we're out of here."

She's not one to let me dwell in my insecurity.

Demi, of course, finds the only strappy heels I own buried in the back of my closet. I can't resist her persistence to try them with the dress.

Recognizing a more obstinate opponent than myself, I put them on then stand in front of the mirror again.

I just can't get over how different I look.

Demi really is a magician.

This sophisticated woman is a stranger.

Taking my hand this time, Demi drags me out to the kitchen to show off her work of art.

I get caught up in the excitement as the women in my kitchen do their best impression of a group of horny men as catcalls reverberate through the house when they see my transformation.

Maybe tonight will be more fun than I originally thought.

Demi – shot glass in hand – tosses it back before slamming the glass on the counter. "Alright ladies let's do this!"

Chapter Ten

Kate

We've been at Dean's Bar for about an hour and the girls are making the most of it. I can hardly keep up with them hopping back and forth between the bar and the dance floor.

I'm currently taking a break at the bar while Demi splits her attention between flirting with Dean and convincing me to take shots with her.

The girl's good. I'll give her that.

She already got Dean's number *and* she's talked me into two shots.

"Dean, give us another round!" Speaking of, here she goes again.

The sexy bartender sets out the shots with a wink aimed her way. I've seen Dean around town since he moved back when his father had a heart attack but we haven't spent any time catching up.

Gossip around town is he worked at a bar in Boston before returning to Frostown. He's attractive with his dark hair and eyes, six feet of lean muscle covered in a swirl of tattoos. He's got ink covering every available inch of exposed skin, and I'm sure there's plenty more hidden beneath his clothes.

"Come on Kate! We're celebrating!" Somehow, the tequila drops what little filter Demi has.

"I didn't know we were celebrating." I'm so confused.

"Silly, we're celebrating our new friendship. You're the first friend I've made since I moved here." She pouts like I should already know this.

Oh, I guess that's a valid reason.

"And then we're getting you laid!"

Choking, I almost inhale the shot I threw back at her declaration.

She's crazy!

She, oh so helpfully, slaps my back when I set off in a coughing fit. When it's apparent I'll survive, she turns me to face the karaoke stage. "Relax, Kate. I'm just teasing."

Thank God! I have no idea how I was going to talk myself out of that one. She's like a dog with a bone when she gets an idea in her head.

If what Jade said is true, I've got more than enough man trouble at the moment, thank you very much.

Speaking of Jade, the ladies from the clubhouse have moved the party on stage, currently belting out an off-key rendition of "Girl's Just Want to Have Fun" by Cyndi Lauper, singing like their lives depend on it.

Demi and I cheer them on like we're front row at the next Grammy award performance.

The ladies give a bow at the end of their performance before hopping off the stage to rejoin us.

The jukebox kicks on signaling the end of this round of karaoke.

Laughing over the loud music, we all move back to the bar for another round.

I decline the shot Jade attempts to thrust in my hand, knowing I need to pace myself or I'll be sloppy drunk in no time.

"Boo! You're no fun!" She sounds just like Demi. She's feeling no pain.

Maybe Demi needs to focus her "friendship" on her instead.

"I'll have another later." I tell her.

Her question is really just a distraction. Jade has been trying to entice me onto the dance floor all night. She takes advantage of finally catching me, snatching my hand to drag me out there with the others.

The girls' carefree attitudes and sensual moves bolster my courage as I lose myself in the deep beat of the music pounding through the speakers. One song leads to another and next thing, I know we've danced through several more songs. My body sways in time with the soulful base.

The pulsing reverberation of the song has all of us shaking our butts. Anyone watching would see an imitation of their last karaoke performance. Girls just having fun.

When the slow pounding beat of the next song starts, I turn to the bar intent on hydrating when the girls show no sign of slowing down.

An overpowering awareness halts my progress before I step off the dance floor.

I search the bar for the reason for the sudden electric charge sizzling over my skin. An arm slides around my waist before I finish my sweep. Butterflies take flight in my belly as that arm tightens until my back collides with a hard chest. I know that arm and the man it belongs to.

There's only one man who sends those tingles racing through my body. Glancing over my shoulder, my eyes get ensnared in blazing blue pools of heat. My assumption is confirmed.

Mac has entered the building.

Chapter Eleven

Mac

I'm running on fumes when we pull up to the clubhouse. We returned early from our run down to the Louisiana charter to check in with the brothers there. Ryker wanted to get back to Frostown as soon as possible, laser focused on ending the drug dealing here. As good as Byte is, we've been unable to find a connection between the victims. And so far, I haven't gotten any useful information from Kate. Not that I've put much effort into it.

Still, I never should have pulled her into this.

Guilt swirls through me again as my thoughts inevitably return to her. I've argued with myself over the past few weeks, mind changing minute to minute. Going back and forth on whether or not I want to see where this attraction between us could go, worried she'd drop me in a hot minute if she discovers why I initially approached her.

But I can't deny that space she occupies in my head. The lust that shoots through me each and every time she enters my thoughts. I've jacked off an embarrassing number of times to images of the desire overwhelming her the night I took her for a ride. That kiss has sparked many a fantasy of spreading her out, having my wicked way with her. So many ways. The possibilities are endless.

It takes me a minute to notice the clubhouse is like a tomb when we walk through the doors.

"Where are the girls?" Looks like Bomber's plan to take one of the girls to his room isn't gonna be happening.

If they even made it that far. None of us are shy about our sexual activities. Some even need the audience to get off.

It's one of my worries about Kate. I'm not sure how receptive she'll be to our lifestyle.

I reach for my phone when it vibrates in my pocket.

Jade: I know u guys r back. Come 2 Deans I have a surprise for u and ur gonna love it

"They must have a sixth sense, Jade said to head to Dean's bar." I leave out the part about her surprise. No clue what that might be.

"Wanna head over there?" Ryker asks.

I'm intrigued by Jade's cryptic words. Already, I'm nodding my head as I head to my room. "Give me ten to shower and change."

I'm in dire need of washing the dirt and grime of the road away.

My brain switches to the drug problems in town as the water pours over my tired body.

What are we missing?

There has to be a connection but fuck me if I could solve the puzzle.

I know Ryker trusts that we'll figure it out. He's relying on me, I don't want to fail him. There usually isn't a problem I can't dissect and solve.

Irritation washes over me as the resolution to this particular mystery eludes me.

My gut tells me Kate isn't involved and has absolutely no knowledge of it. I worry I may have inadvertently pulled her right smack into the middle of this shit.

My dick hardens as I imagine more pleasurable activities with her. Like getting her under me. Wondering what will be revealed when I finally get her out of those conservative clothes. Clothes that I know, without a doubt, hide a banging body.

I rush through my shower, ignoring my hard dick. Those fuckers will leave without me if I don't hurry.

Dressed in faded blue jeans and a plain black t-shirt, I'm pulling my jacket over my shoulders on my way to the main room where the brothers are about to walk out the door.

"Let's roll." Ryker calls. Not that he waits for a reply, he's out the door before he even finishes speaking.

Prez is a take no shit kinda guy. Expects his orders to be followed. Not just because of his title. He earns the respect of every member of the club on the daily.

After finding space for our bikes a couple doors down from Dean's Bar, we dismount and head inside.

Eyes adjusting to the dim light, I see my "surprise" right away. Looks like Jade is playing matchmaker. I would be lying if I said I wasn't happy about it.

My eyes are glued to the ladies on the dance floor. So lost in their fun they haven't noticed us yet. One lady in particular holds me spellbound.

I watch Kate in this unguarded moment. Watch her let loose on the dance floor, captivated by this rare occurrence. She moves with a natural sensuality, drawing the interested gazes of every fucker in the bar. Including my brothers.

Unfortunately for them, they're gonna find out how far I'm willing to go if any of them hit on her.

For a minute, all I can do is stand there watching her. The painted on black dress might as well be a spotlight magnifying her beauty. It puts her trim body clearly on display for every motherfucker in here to see.

I catch teasing glimpses of her tits rising just above the neckline. There is no hope of controlling the slide of my gaze down the silky black material, over her trim thighs to sexy black heels.

Lust ignites as I stop momentarily to admire the way her dress hugs the curve of her ass. The skirt's hem teases her thighs like a lover's caress.

I adjust myself, hands itching to replace the material. Imagine grazing my fingers along the soft skin of her toned thighs right to the paradise hidden beneath. Of pushing my hands under that skirt to spread her wide, exposing her wet little pussy for the first time.

She looks like sin in that scrap of fabric.

Joker's voice breaks me out of my fantasy. "Man, how did I not know how hot she is?"

He's gonna be a dead man if he doesn't heed my warning look. Even through my red haze, his smirk is telling, I fell right into his trap. Doesn't mean I'm not still contemplating putting my fist through his face.

Mistaking my stillness for hesitation, a slap to my back pushes me toward the dance floor. And what I'm finally admitting. At least to myself.

Kate is the girl of my dreams.

Any intention of backing off, of being the good guy – fleeting as the thought was – leaves the building when I put eyes back on her dancing form.

She is stunning. Her lack of inhibition in the safety of her group of friends is intoxicating. And I'm the lucky bastard about to reap the benefits.

"Go get her brother. I got my eye on something else." Ridiculously shaking his hips, Joker dances his way to the group of ladies. He slides between Josie and Raquel, forcing his way to the center of the group. His goal apparently the curvy blond I don't recognize.

While I could appreciate the stranger's beauty, she's no comparison to the woman I have in my sights.

I circle the group to approach Kate from the back, momentarily distracted from my mission by the sexy sway of her hips. Shaking my mind out of the gutter, I step up behind her, sliding my arm around her waist.

My hand slips easily over the silky material covering her stomach. With a firm press of my hand, I exert enough pressure to pull her back against my hard chest.

Her tantalizing body is a perfect fit to my own.

My beard brushes the smooth skin of her cheek as I lean down to be heard in the loud bar. My voice a husky growl torn from my chest. "Wanna dance?"

She sasses back even as she turns in my arms. "I think we already are."

Her teasing tone goes directly to my dick. All blood flows south.

Fuck. Her sass is sexy.

A surge of satisfaction courses through me, realizing I'm breaking through her timid walls to the beauty within.

"Just wanted to make sure. I don't want to make any assumptions with you." There is no way to hide the arousal roughening my voice.

I test her comfort level, sliding my thigh between hers, forcing her to spread her legs to accommodate me. She doesn't protest when my hard muscles press firmly to her pussy. Tightening my arms, I pull her impossibly closer until her tits plump up against my chest. Her nipples strain against that black silk with each panting breath.

She's a natural fit in my arms. I slip a hand down her back to rest above the swell of her ass, rubbing sensual circles on her lower back. With my other hand, I can't resist playing with the curls she's left hanging down her back.

The wild strands are as silky as I imagined and only add to her allure.

A complex mix of innocence and sin, wrapped in an irresistible package I have no hope of resisting.

My thigh pushes closer to her core as thoughts of defiling her innocence, dirtying her up, consume me. I bury my face in her hair in an attempt to regain some semblance of control.

No idea how long we stay locked together, the spell I'm weaving to build her desire has snared me too.

A bump from my back intrudes. I watch the sexual fog clear from her eyes as Josie's voice comes from behind me.

"Mac! I'm so glad you're back!" Josie rubs her tits on my back in an attempt to entice me away from the woman in my arms.

Irritated with the interruption, I don't even look at her. "Get lost, Josie. We're dancing."

But it's too late. I watch as Kate withdraws physically – and mentally.

She turns to the curvy blond I don't recognize and whispers something in her ear. The blond immediately grabs her hand, towing her off the dance floor.

I stand here like a dumbass as I helplessly watch them expertly weave through the crowd to the bar.

I barely spare Josie a glance. "Back off, Josie. Go find another idiot to play with. I'm not interested."

Not giving her another second, I leave her fuming on the dance floor to catch up to Kate.

Like a puppy trailing its master, I take the same path to the bar as Kate and her friend. Catching up in time to hear the blond order shots of tequila.

Surrounded on both sides, men blatantly check them out. Jealousy explodes. It's a foreign feeling. One I don't have the time to examine more closely.

I make eye contact with the asshole on the stool next to them, motioning for him to get lost. He puts his life at risk when he ignores my deadly glare. Instead, he makes the mistake of hitting on my woman.

What the fuck? My woman?

Where the hell did that thought come from?

The douche finally makes his only intelligent decision of the night – slinking off the stool – moving on to his next round of disappointment.

Satisfied, I slide onto the vacant stool and reach across the bar to snag one of the shots Dean sets in front of the ladies. The friend doesn't even notice. She's too caught up batting her lashes at Dean behind the bar.

I throw back the shot. The burn in my throat nothing compared to the emerald fire lighting Kate's eyes. What she doesn't know, it does nothing but add to the desire igniting my blood.

Taking my chances, I grin down at the adorable fierceness in front of me. I don't resist the urge to touch her. It's useless, so why even try? I pull her close until she's standing between my thighs just to watch that fire burn brighter.

It's not only her I'm tormenting. There is no way to hide my hard dick rubbing against her.

Her friend reaches her hand between us. It breaks our staring contest for now.

"Hi! You must be Mac. I'm Demi." The blond introduces herself. "I've heard a lot about you."

I take her hand. "Yeah. Nice to meet you. What have you heard about me?"

See, I can be polite when necessary.

I'm more interested in knowing what she's heard and from where. Hopefully not the clubhouse.

I haven't seen her around town in the months we've lived here but that doesn't mean anything. I could have run into her anywhere. Petite blonds weren't really an anomaly around here. She may be pretty but it was the brunette in my arms that captivates me.

"We didn't expect to see you guys this weekend. Didn't you cancel your plans with Kate?" Hmm, so she's heard about me from Kate.

The pink hue staining Kate's cheeks confirms that theory. It's always a good sign when the woman you want is talking about you with her friends.

"Yeah. Plans changed. Weren't supposed to be back until Sunday but something came up. I wasn't expecting to see Kate out tonight."

Feeling Kate's body stiffen against me, I gently rub my fingers in soothing circles where my hand rests on her stomach. It takes a minute but she eventually relaxes back against me. Her exhaled sigh ghosts over the side of my neck and does absolutely nothing to calm my still hard dick.

I sit back, watching in fascination as Demi teases Kate out of her shell like a blooming flower. Her escalating outrageousness apparent as she throws out ridiculous come on lines to help loosen my girl up. I appreciate the effort she's putting in. She is working hard to keep Kate giggling as much as she's blushing. Kate's blush keeps me on a razor's edge of desire. I have to suppress the urge to rip off her dress. If only to see how far down that pink hue stains her skin.

Hell, who am I kidding? What I really want is to follow that blush down and taste every inch of her delectable skin.

I'm pulled from my fantasy as Demi keeps talking. I gotta say the girl is a multitasker. Splitting her focus between us and flirting with Dean behind the bar.

Girl's got game.

The brothers interrupt when they gather around us.

No shame in her game, Demi blatantly checks them out too.

I wonder which of the brothers caught her attention.

She turns to make eye contact with the woman in my arms. Shrugging unrepentantly, she mouths "Yummy."

Kate's body shakes against mine. A giggle wracking her body at her friend's outrageousness. She's given me all her weight, gone completely pliant in my arms.

Rightness settles in my soul at the positive turn my night has taken.

"Brother, we're out. Gonna head back to the clubhouse." Ryker's words are for me but his eyes are all for Demi. She is exactly his type. Petite curvy blond with attitude.

He has yet to see the attitude. I'm looking forward to that scene. I just hope I am around to see it.

Although, I am a little surprised at his blatant perusal. Prez is discreet. Always has been. And his next words are a shock.

"Do you ladies want to join us? A group of us are gonna continue the party there."

A silent conversation passes between Kate and Demi. It's fascinating to watch before Kate shakes her head at her friend.

"I need to get home. Demi, you go, have fun." It's not surprising when she declines.

Demi's interested gaze locks on Ryker. "Lead the way, big guy."

I instinctively understand Kate isn't ready for more, so it's time to take her home. Linking our fingers, I lead her out to my bike where I strap my helmet on her head. I only have the one since I wasn't expecting company.

"What about you?" She asks.

"I'm good. It's a short drive." I reassure her.

Climbing on the bike, I help her mount behind me so she can retain as much dignity as possible in that dress. I take off for the short drive to her house with her arms wrapped tightly around me.

Chapter Twelve

Mac

I'm an idiot.

I make the mistake of planting a steamy kiss on Kate's lips when I walk her to her door. Now it's torturous to even consider leaving her. Her responsiveness makes it damn near impossible to walk away.

My only consolation is her promise to call the next day, already impatient to see her again.

Leaving her house once she's safely inside, I ride to the clubhouse, backing my bike into my usual spot then heading inside. The party is in full swing when I enter the main room.

Before I can take a step towards the bar, I catch sight of Byte waiting for me across the room. He nods his head for me to follow him before disappearing down the hallway. Trailing behind, I enter his room to the bright light of the numerous monitors all lit up, casting a blue hue on the opposite wall.

I have no clue how he keeps track of everything happening on them.

Taking a seat, he waves me into the chair next to his desk where a folder sits unopened. "I found a connection."

Apprehension settles in my gut as I brace myself for what I'm about to hear.

"There's a trucker that's been flashing a lot of cash around the casinos out of state. Too much cash for a trucker's salary. Plus, he has a wife and kids to support."

"What's his connection to the victims?" I don't see it but I wait for him to spell it out for me.

"There's only one and you're not gonna like it." He warns before continuing. "He has a cousin that works at the high school. He's a teacher too."

"He works with Kate?" I really don't like where this is going. That feeling of foreboding grows with every word out of my brother's mouth.

"Yeah man." Byte confirms. "He teaches American History. Name's Michael Smith."

Cursing, I finally glance at the folder in front of me. I flip it open to a background check on one Vince "Vinny" DeLuca.

The report shows a history of past due bills and a pending foreclosure on the house he shares with his wife and kids.

Piece of shit not taking care of his family.

"Son of a bitch isn't using that money to take care of his family." Assholes like him just piss me off.

"I know, man. He's a piece of shit for sure. From what I've been able to find, he's been cheating on the wife for years. No idea why she's stayed so long. Only two things make sense. She's either afraid to leave or can't afford to. I think it's lack of funds. She doesn't work. Stays home to take care of the kids.

"He's a fixture in the casinos in Mississippi but he hasn't shown his face there lately either. Word is, he's into a shark for a lot of money. I looked into his financials and he doesn't have the cash to pay him back. I think he found somewhere neutral to hide out."

Disgusted, I throw the file on his desk. Casino gambling is illegal in the state of Tennessee. The fact he's crossing state lines to get his fix just makes it that much harder to track him down. He must have burned himself in the closer casinos to be traveling as far as Mississippi.

"So, what now?" I ask.

"Ryker sent Bomber and Joker to pay him a visit at his house." Seeing my surprise, Byte goes on to explain. "I think Prez had an ulterior motive with Joker. Last I saw, Ryker was about to beat the shit out of him when Joker was flirting with the blond that came back to the clubhouse with him. Rock and Bomb were stepping between them when I gave him the update."

I can't contain my laugh at Joker's expense. I know in my gut Joker is playing with fire but the brother has never been afraid to get burned. And here I thought it would be the tiny blond handing Ryker his ass.

I lose my humor as I refocus on our issue. "They still gone?"

Byte nods. "Yeah, I don't expect they'll be back for a while. DeLuca's house is about an hour north of here."

Holding my fist out for a bump, I leave Byte to his computers. Kate consumes my thoughts again before I even make it through the doorway.

This new lead just adds to my growing concern for her safety. Wary of potential danger in a place where she should feel safe behind the fences of the school. I doubt a teacher would take the chance to harm another on school grounds but I'm not taking chances. I need to figure out a way to keep her safe.

Reentering the main room, I catch sight of Ryker at the bar with Demi. From the quick glance I shoot their way, it doesn't look like my brother is gonna be getting lucky tonight.

No, poor guy looks to be getting his ass handed to him as I pass them on my way to the kitchen. I'm gonna keep my ass as far from that as possible. I don't need their drama causing issues for me.

I reach in the fridge for a bottle of water, gulping it down before tossing the empty in the trash. Deciding to call it a night, I bump into Josie on my way back out of the kitchen.

"There you are, Mac. Come on, we didn't get a chance to dance earlier. I missed you." Her arms latch onto me like an octopus looking for its next victim.

I hate this shit.

Working to disentangle myself from Josie, I catch a quick flash of blond in the doorway before it disappears.

"Josie, stop. I already told you no." Now I'm pissed.

By the time I escape the kitchen, Demi was already storming out the clubhouse doors.

"Fuck."

There's no better word for what my situation just turned into.

Chapter Thirteen

Kate

I walk through the doors of Sweet Treats Saturday morning with a pep in my step. My stomach has been growling since I decided to come here this morning, full on salivating in anticipation of the baked goodies in my near future.

Demi stands behind the counter cashing out a customer.

She waves me over to a table in the corner, her normal early morning cheer subdued.

Hmm, maybe she had a long night.

It didn't take long after we met that first day to establish a routine. My work schedule perfectly aligns with her hours at the bakery, so we meet a few times a week right as she's closing.

I wait for her to join me at our table with my favorite coffee and croissant.

True to form, she plops down a few minutes later.

"Good morning." I greet my friend while simultaneously reaching for my coffee.

"Girl, you missed out last night." Demi can't hide her wary expression.

Well, that doesn't bode well for me.

There is only one reason she could be uncomfortable telling me and that reason is the man I've been spending time with.

"What happened?" I'm not sure I really want to know but there's no sense burying my head in the sand. Besides, Demi would never allow that.

"So, you know I went back to the clubhouse with Ryker." She doesn't wait for a response. "After he dropped you off, Mac came back to the clubhouse. He was snuggled up with that bitch Josie when I saw him."

Sharp hurt is a knife slicing through me, unbidden images of Mac with another woman popping in my head. More so, that it's the woman that has been going out of her way to make me uncomfortable.

And right after he dropped me off last night. I guess it's a good thing I didn't do more than kiss him. Believe me, the thought of inviting him in definitely crossed my mind.

"Probably for the best. I never believed I could hold the attention of a man like him." I attempt to brush it off.

Don't let her see your pain.

Demi lays her hand over mine, showing a softer side I didn't think her capable of.

"You are a catch, Kate. Don't let any man tell you any different. He would be lucky to have a gem like you as his woman." I fight back tears at her encouraging words.

With that one statement, Demi shows me exactly why I took a chance befriending her.

I'm not blind to the fact that Mac and I are night and day but her words give me a new outlook. They change my perspective and I just know I will be alright.

With a friend like her, how could I not be?

A subject change is in order. "So, you and Ryker, huh?"

Her vigorous scoff echoes through the bakery.

She about threw herself out of her chair with that one.

"Yeah, I don't think so. He may be hot but he's under the mistaken impression that he's God's gift to women. I left him high and dry when he interrupted my good time with Joker. After I gave him a piece of my mind, of course."

"Of course." I think my friend is protesting a little too much. But I'm not going to call her on it. I think I'll sit back and watch the show.

Although, I am a little sad I missed what sounds like an interesting night. Demi left with Ryker but then she was flirting with Joker?

I'm not sure I want to know how that went down.

I may not call her out but I let a sly smile cross my face. "So, are you going to see him again?"

With a cackle she asks, "Which one?"

My friend is nothing if not a flirt. She doesn't take men seriously. Choosing instead to focus on making her shop successful and turning a profit. Men are a pastime for her.

We spend the rest of the morning chatting about the shenanigans the ladies got up to at the bar. By the time I leave the bakery, my heart is lighter, my cheeks hurt from all the laughter Demi pulled from me. But it's a good kind of hurt. Food for the soul.

I know, without a doubt, Demi's outrageousness was more over the top than usual. I truly appreciate her dedication to driving Mac from my thoughts. Even if only for a short time.

* * *

Taking the last of the laundry out of the dryer, I carry the basket to my bedroom. The doorbell rings right as I place it in my closet.

I have no idea who would stop by without calling, but really not surprised to find Mac on my doorstep when I swing the door open.

Once again, with that sexy lean against the doorframe. It takes effort to lock my knees against a swoon. "What are you doing here?"

My hold on the handle is the only thing keeping me upright in the face of the intensity in his blue eyes. His short hair stands on end like he's been running his fingers through it. Maybe in agitation.

"You didn't answer my calls or texts. Didn't really give me a choice but to come check on you."

Unable to hide my guilty expression, I know he's been trying to reach me all day. I've ignored them all. Not ready to face the inevitable brush off.

"I've been busy." I lie.

He makes no effort to hide the disbelief on his face. Clearly, he doesn't believe me. "May I come in?"

Manners winning out, I step away from the door and hold it open for him. I know he won't let me avoid the conversation he's intent on having.

He walks in like he owns the place. Goosebumps break out on my skin where his arm brushes against me. He doesn't stop until he reaches the middle of the living room, his overwhelming presence sucks all the oxygen out of the room.

He's an imposing form in his standard worn out jeans, vest, motorcycle boots and black t-shirt as he takes in my home for the first time.

April and I have made a lot of changes since my father died. The once cold and formal home has been transformed into a cozy and inviting haven I cherish.

The fireplace is the main focal point of the room, framed by the soft tan sofa and loveseat we love to curl up in on gloomy days. The rarely used television is mounted above the fireplace, a larger size unnecessary in this female household. Mac takes it all in with one sweeping glance before zeroing back in on me.

Resigned to the uncomfortable conversation, the manners ingrained in me rear their ugly head yet again. "Would you like something to drink?"

There. Polite but not too nice.

But he wouldn't be the Mac I've come to know if he didn't jump right in to address the elephant in the room.

"Nothing happened with Josie at the clubhouse last night. I know what Demi thinks she saw in the kitchen probably didn't look good, but I promise you, I didn't do anything with her."

His words circle in my head, I don't know what to believe.

Demi is adamant about what she saw. Mac and Josie getting cozy before she interrupted.

But is that really what it was?

Could she have misunderstood the situation? Am I an idiot to even consider believing him?

My silence must last too long because he keeps talking as he stalks across the room, invading my personal space.

"I really like you, Kate. I think there's something special between us and I don't want to lose it over a misunderstanding." His words sound sincere.

I'm torn.

Even if I do believe that nothing happened last night, what are the chances he won't run into temptation in the future? I've already given him a small piece of myself. How much worse will it feel if it happens down the road?

How long can my boring self really hold his attention? I won't lie. That right there is my biggest fear.

"Mac, we're so different. I think we'd be better off as friends."

He's shaking his head before I even finish my sentence. Moving right up into my personal space, the warmth of his palms cup my face. Electricity sparks just like every other time he touches me.

"Kate, I want to be more than your friend. I can't seem to get you out of my head. No matter how hard I try, you're right there." Moving closer, his next words whisper over my lips. "You consume me. I want to go to sleep and wake up every day with you in my arms. Believe me when I say, you are the only woman I want."

His words rock me to my core. They also prove I don't stand a chance in this battle of wills.

He is my own temptation I have no hope of resisting. Maybe it's time I give myself a chance at happiness.

Unable to nod my head with his firm grip on my face, I take a chance and pray he doesn't break my heart. "Okay. We can try this again."

Gentling his hold, he presses his mouth to mine, sweeping me away in a scorching kiss.

I feel his touch through my entire body, even though our only connection is his lips on mine, hands holding my face so tenderly. It's more so a gentle melding of his mouth to mine but no less toe curling than a tongue dueling battle.

Ending the contact far too soon, he presses his forehead to mine. "You won't regret this."

"You better mean that." I warn him.

"I do." With one last quick press of his lips to mine he pushes for more. "Hoping like hell you'd agree, I brought your helmet. Go for a ride with me."

Knowing I'm not going to win this round either – not that I really want to – I nod then head to my bedroom to change.

We walk out the door hand in hand, our fingers entwined in a natural move as he leads me to his motorcycle. Like always, he secures my helmet before once again assisting me on the bike.

This time he doesn't have to prompt me to wrap my arms around him. There is no hesitation as I wind my arms around his sides, giving into the desire to tease his abs before pressing my hands to the material of his shirt. His muscles clench deliciously within my grip.

Then I hold on tight. My breasts plastered to the back of this strong sexy man who effortlessly controls the rumbling beast beneath us.

Chapter Fourteen

Kate

The vibe of this ride feels different from the others. Before he was cautious of my inexperience on a motorcycle. This time when we reach the end of Main Street, Mac revs the engine before shooting off down the open road much faster than before.

The loud rumble of the motor vibrates through my entire body.

His control of the machine is sexy. Reaching down with one hand, he gives a reassuring squeeze to my thigh pressed tight to his hard muscles. A confident assurance that he knows that he's got me.

Euphoria floods me as we fly down the open road. The newfound feeling of freedom is as unfamiliar as it is intoxicating as I hang on for the ride of my life.

Never in my life have I felt as carefree as I do with the wind whipping my hair while holding tight to the sexy man in front of me. He handles the machine with the expertise of a seasoned rider.

So lost in my newfound freedom, it takes a minute to notice he's pulled off the road. Setting his feet on the ground for balance, Mac kicks down the stand then offers me his helping hand.

I cling to him as I climb off, unsteadiness in my legs expected this time.

My eyes scan the unfamiliar clearing we're in, no idea where we are.

I might not recognize the area but the people I do. Mac's brothers are scattered around a roaring fire pit about twenty feet from the edge of the lake.

Still holding his hand, I turn to Mac with an inquisitive look. "Where are we?"

"This is Danger's land. He has a cabin about a hundred yards up that way." He explains.

I see nothing when my eyes track the direction he points.

Everything beyond the thick trees around us is shrouded in complete darkness.

Don't ask me to try to find it. I'd be lost in no time.

And it's not only the darkness beyond the fire light. Add in my awful sense of direction and I couldn't find my way there if my life depended on it.

"I'll have to take your word for it. I can't see a thing." I admit.

His deep laugh is irresistible. It's the first time I've heard the sound from him. Of course, it can be added to his long list of impossibly sexy qualities.

The husky sound grinds out from his chest and is just as sexy as the rest of him. Like his motorcycle, the sound rumbles right to my core. Unexpectedly, cream escapes to soak my panties.

Not sure why you're surprised. Everything he does is hot.

While I'm caught up with my inner voice, he leads me over to the group of men sitting around the fire pit.

I haven't spent much time with Mac's brothers. If I'm going to give this thing between us a real chance then I need to get comfortable in their presence, intimidating as it is.

"Babe, you remember everyone?" He asks.

Blushing at the endearment, I nod a greeting to all the men. Words freeze in my throat as my sight adjusts to the darkness surrounding us.

Then I wish it hadn't.

My eyes about pop out of my head when I catch movement just beyond the fire light.

The silhouette of a couple locked in an erotic embrace enthralls me. The flames of the dancing fire offer alluring glimpses that captivate me.

Danger holds a topless Raquel caged against a tree. His mouth attacks a nipple while he twists the other between his fingers. Though it looks torturous, Raquel's moans dispute that thought.

I'm a voyeur incapable of tearing my eyes from the erotic sight as a shirtless Danger pushes her hand into the opening of his unzipped jeans. The groan tearing from his throat vibrates against her breast when I imagine her hand has wrapped around his hardness.

Hypnotized, I am completely incapable of tearing my eyes from the eroticism playing out in front of me. So wrapped up in what they're doing, I can't even think to be embarrassed when more wetness soaks my panties.

Reality intrudes on my voyeurism when Mac slides his hand down over my hip. The firm squeeze tears my gaze from the erotic couple.

He waits until my eyes meet his before lowering his head to brush his lips teasingly over my mouth. Like our ride here, this kiss is different from the others we've shared.

Mac weaves an intoxicating spell. He knows exactly how to drive thoughts of everyone and everything else out of my head.

The sensual play of his lips spurs me to chase his mouth for more. Reversing his retreat, his tongue licks along the seam of my lips demanding entry, while using his hold on my hip to pull me flush to his hard body.

My breasts rub against the hard muscles of his pecs as I squirm uncontrollably, his hard chest teasing my nipples.

All the while his mouth continues its torture.

My woeful inexperience is no match to the skillful mouth ravaging mine. With sharp nips of his teeth, he coaxes my mouth open, taking full advantage of my gasp to invade.

My hands have a mind of their own as they glide up his hard chest to wrap around his neck. The move gives me more leverage to shamelessly press my breasts closer, the lace of my bra abrading my sensitive nipples. It's a biting contrast that adds to my sensual fog.

Between the erotic show in front of us, Mac's kisses, and my body's response – it's all a sensual assault I have no hope to fight.

Whimpers I have no hope of containing pour from my mouth to his until Mac kisses a trail to my jaw. No longer muffled, my moans float out into the dark night with his mouth no longer there to capture them.

Mac knows exactly what to do to build my desire even higher, alternating teasing bites with gentle sucks to my neck.

"Mac." His name is nothing more than a sigh from my lips.

I'm ensnared by the heat lighting his eyes when he lifts his head. "I want you."

My core clenches at his whispered words.

My fog of lust lifts with his head. I bury my face between his hard pecs when I remember the other men are still present. From the look of it, they've been shamelessly watching the show we put on.

"I can't. Not here." I'm not saying no.

I know. It surprises the heck out of me too.

It's not like I'm a complete virgin. I also can't lie to myself. My one disappointing experience is no match for the man exuding sensuality in front of me. So easily does he make me lose my head.

"Can we go somewhere else?" Self-doubt returns as the sensual spell lifts.

No doubt he sees my hesitation.

Even I could hear the uncertainty in my voice.

Chapter Fifteen

Mac

A vise tightens somewhere in the vicinity of my heart at the hesitancy of her question.

What the hell was that about?

I don't realize my expression softens until her emerald eyes brighten. The shimmering fire expresses what she is unable to convey in her words. Her desire may be overwhelming but she's right here with me.

I would give this woman the world for that look right there.

I catch Joker's laughing face when I disentangle from her gaze. "Coming up for air, brother?"

The bark of laughter is apparently the wrong thing to do. That's made obvious from the pain in my side where Kate's fingers dig into my flesh.

My surprised gaze flies back to hers as I jerk away from the pain. My mouth spreads in a wide grin at the fierce scowl aimed right back at me.

"Minx." I can't help teasing her just to watch a blush steal over her cheeks when she realizes what she's done and is now the focus of all my brothers amusement. She's an adorable mix of fierceness and embarrassment, with a side of lingering arousal. The arousing dichotomy sparks quicksilver in my veins like a bolt of lightning.

We are gonna light the world on fire when we finally get between the sheets. Or on any flat surface.

I'm not picky.

Those thoughts do nothing to ease my still hard dick. No, instead it jerks against her stomach where it's trapped between us.

"Hey girl, don't sweat it. We were all enjoying the show." Joker, or Jackass as I like to call him, continues his teasing.

The brother never knows when to quit.

"Jackass." The sound of Ryker's slap to the back of his head sounds the same time as his voice. Apparently, I'm not the only one who calls him that.

"Thanks, Prez. She's gonna bolt if I let her go." He's lucky I don't want to lose the ground I've gained with Kate or I would have done it myself.

And I wouldn't have stopped there. No, I would have beat the shit out of him. The only other thing stopping me is instinctively knowing Kate would hate it and I do not want to risk scaring her away just when I have her back in my arms. I pull a chair close to the fire, at the same time using my hold on Kate to pull her down on my lap.

Shifting the focus off my girl, I bullshit with my brothers to give her some time to get over her embarrassment. Not that she has any reason to feel embarrassed. None of us will judge.

It takes some time but she eventually relaxes back into me as the conversation flows around her.

She's just taking it all in. The quiet woods surrounding us, the fire playing in front of us, and the easy conversation with my brothers.

Contentment like I have never felt before settles in my soul. I never thought life could get much better since joining the MC but this right here is damn near perfect.

"Mac says you're a teacher? Do you like that?" I tune back into the conversation when I hear Ryker's question.

"It's okay. My father didn't give me much of a choice. I really can't complain though. It pays the bills." The fact she's sharing her true feelings on it, it's obvious she's getting more comfortable around my brothers.

I have been through hell and back with these men. They would have my back no matter what. Just like I would them. As my chosen family, it is essential the woman in my life accepts them.

"So, you know the club's been investigating the overdoses and who has been selling them the drugs?" Damn Ryker for bringing this up.

He knows I was dragging my feet about pulling her further into our investigation. He's deliberately taking the decision out of my hands.

There is no way she misses my stiffening body beneath hers.

She answers his question while giving me a quizzical look. "Yes. Mac mentioned it. I wish there was something I could do to help."

"There might be something. Do you know Michael Smith? He works at the school with you." He presses.

"Not really. I know who he is but I've never talked to him. Do you think he's involved?" She asks.

"We don't know for sure." Ryker answers her question. "He has a connection to a possible suspect we're looking into."

"I can try talking to him. See if there's anything I can find out for you guys." She offers.

"No, babe. I don't want you getting involved." My words grind out, rough with the fear of putting her in danger, a warning meant more for Ryker than Kate. *The last thing she needs to be doing is putting herself in danger for us.*

"Mac, I want to help." While a part of me admires her insistence to help, it's overwhelmed by my need to keep her as far away from danger as possible.

I do *not* want her anywhere near potential suspects. Just the thought of putting her in harm's way freezes my blood.

It's my greatest fear. Failing to protect her in a dangerous situation we put her in.

"Let me be clear." Ryker rolls on while that fear paralyzes my vocal cords. "We do not want you doing anything to put yourself at risk. If you think of or see anything, you tell Mac. You do not do anything to put a target on your back."

It was the best I would get for now. Prez isn't gonna put innocents at risk but if there is any way to use the situation to our advantage, he will take it.

She agrees and I promise myself I will do everything in my power to protect her. The conversation takes another turn with Ryker's next question. "What would you do if you had the chance to do anything?"

My family is starting to accept her. Prez is no bullshitter. He wouldn't worry about hiding his dislike if he had a problem with her. He wouldn't show an interest in her either. That acceptance reassures me they'll protect her as one of our own if anything were to happen.

"If I could do anything? I've always loved helping people in need. I do what I can volunteering in the community but I wish I could do more." Ducking her head to hide her face in my shoulder, we can all see she surprised herself with her honesty.

No man here would make a joke about voicing her dreams. It will take some time but she'll learn that.

"Growing up my mom had a neighbor that helped us out when she could. My mom had MS. It got bad when I was young. Too small to do much. It would have been a big help if she had someone like you to help." It isn't often Rocker talks about his past – or really much at all – so when he does, we all stop and pay attention. His words seem to get to my girl.

She glows as her shyness disappears. "Yes! There are so many people that need a little bit of help but not enough to qualify for aid. If I could help those people and-"

She abruptly cuts herself off.

"And what?" We're all interested in what she has to say. Doesn't seem to be something she's used to.

"Sorry, I could talk about this for hours. I'm probably boring you guys."

"Not at all. I think it's a great idea. What else were you going to say?" I'm grateful to my friend for pushing her. Ryker putting in the effort to bring her into the fold is important.

"It's just, I'd really like to be able to start a shelter too. Or something to help women and people in abusive or unsafe situations. I think a lot of people get so isolated they feel stuck in a crappy situation. I wish there were more places out there to help those in need."

This woman continues to amaze me. My girl has a big heart, wanting to help wherever she sees a need.

It's also an idea similar to what the MC has been considering. When we moved to Frostown, we wanted to find a way to make a difference in the community but we haven't settled on anything yet. This might be something that will work for us. I'll have to talk to Ryker to see what we can do.

The conversation shifts again, the brothers take pity on her embarrassment from sharing so much of herself.

What she doesn't realize – her passion is sexy in the way it lights her from within.

I see the interest on some of my brothers' faces. None of us are looking to settle down but sometimes that shit just smacks you in the face. You gotta roll with the punches to get where you want to be. Or in this case, get who you want to get.

Although, there's a different kind of interest on Joker's face. The brother is just horny but smart enough to redirect his attention – knowing he'll deserve an ass beating for getting a hard-on over my girl's enthusiasm.

Speaking of hard-ons. My own. *Not* my friends. It's about time for some privacy. I have shared women with my brothers more times than I care to count. Kate is different. I am definitely not ready to share her. That's just not something I'll ever be willing to do.

Even if my brothers didn't participate, there is no way my girl is ready to put on a show. She may have a little voyeurism in her but something tells me exhibitionism just isn't her thing.

Ready to get her alone, I give a quick tap to her hip to stand then pull her right back to my side as soon as I'm vertical. The need to be close to her overwhelms me. To feel her tight body pressed right up to mine. Her hand slips over my stomach as I tower over her slight form. She fits perfectly against my side.

"We're gonna head out." I tell my brothers. "Later."

"Later brother." Their voices echo around the fire.

I lift my chin to the group then guide Kate back to my bike. She squeezes in behind me and I don't even need to prompt her to wrap her arms around me anymore.

Shooting off into the night, I make a split-second decision and head to the clubhouse. While I'm sure she would most likely be more comfortable in her own bed – April being there will be a distraction. She'll be too worried about her hearing us to really let go.

The plans I have will require a hundred percent of her focus.

Chapter Sixteen

Mac

The ride to the clubhouse is a short one. Her hand sliding into mine to dismount the bike becoming so natural, I doubt she even notices the trust she places in me now.

Swinging my leg off my bike, our fingers entwine as we navigate the parking lot. The clubhouse is quiet when we enter. Everyone in the club enjoying the cool night at Danger's.

"Should we have a drink first?" Her uncertainty is back and that just won't do. Using the hold I still have on her hand, I pull her flush to my body again, her softness a perfect fit to my hard muscles. I cannot wait to feel her like this without the barrier of our clothes. The images harden my dick even more.

"If you don't want to do this tonight, just say the word. I want you but I'm in no rush. Remember we're going at your pace." Her radiant smile is my undoing. It lights her up from the inside out. I can't resist pressing a quick kiss to her lips. When I lift my head, her hand clenches mine, her face clear of all uncertainty. "No, I'm good."

"Okay, but you tell me if you want to stop at any time." This is all about her. What she wants, the pace she's willing to move at. I will wait however long she needs to.

Tightening my hold on her hand, our boots echo in the empty room as we cross the floor, heading to the hallway that leads to the back of the building.

As soon as we enter my room, I lose what little control I was hanging on to, pushing her back to the closed door. My forearms rest on either side of her head, caging her against it. I lean in slowly for another kiss, dragging out the anticipation when what I really want to do is devour this woman.

My patience rewarded when she reaches up to chase my teasing mouth. Her eagerness says more than words ever could and is exactly what I was waiting for. She is right here with me. I give in to my desire, devouring her mouth with single-minded focus.

My dick, having calmed down on the ride here, surges back to full hardness. My chest rubs her tits tantalizingly slow even as I hold my hips back from her body. It would be game over as soon as my dick touched her. Even through the layer of our clothes.

I nip her plump lower lip to coax her to open for more. Taking full advantage of a moan parting her lips, I slip my tongue in to duel with hers. The intoxicating taste of her, her sweet scent, invades my senses, quickly dragging me to the brink.

Unable to resist, I smooth my hand down the silky soft skin of her arm. My fingers circle the fluttering pulse in her wrist before sliding to her waist and feathering back up her side to cup her breast.

The swollen curve is a perfect fit in my hand as she arches her back, pressing the supple flesh harder to the palm of my hand, silently begging for more.

My kiss swallows another wanton moan, our tongues tangle in an erotic dance. With teasing licks and sharp bites, I trace my mouth over her jaw, her moans spurring me on as I roam down the column of her neck.

Each gasp of pleasure drawn from her chest a victory. As she loses herself in our erotic play, I increase the pressure of my hand on the fullness of her tit.

So many things I want to do to her. For her. Make her scream and beg for.

I fight the urge to tear off her clothes and feast on her gorgeous body. Barely keeping myself in check, I tease the pad of my thumb back and forth over her nipple.

Her gasping breath snaps my control. Unable to keep my dick from the perfection of her body, I give her my full weight, continuing my forward momentum until I have her completely trapped against the door. My weeping dick seeks the heat of her pussy, it's impossible to miss how wound up she has me.

Without breaking our connection, I turn her away from the door, drawing her across the room, searching blindly for my bed. My legs find the mattress where I drop down and pull her between my spread thighs. She fits perfectly in the space between my legs. My mouth salivates with her tits at the perfect level to play.

Need overwhelms me as I take in the intoxicating vision in front of me. Lips swollen from my kisses, lids at half mast, her emerald eyes glow down at me with need matching my own.

Fuck, but she's beautiful.

I pull her close, burying my face between the paradise of her breasts, her scent once again overwhelming my senses like a Siren's call. I lean back just far enough to watch my fingers torture a nipple. The hard bud visible even through the shirt hiding it from my view.

Gasping breaths my reward, I can't resist teasing her. "Do you like that?"

Her eager nod, the pressure of her pushing the supple flesh further into my palm. She can't hide her desire.

Not to deprive the other, my mouth finds her nipple through the layers of her clothes, closing around it with a hard suck. Her hips circle unconsciously, seeking a fullness in her pussy she's too far gone to realize she's searching for.

The need to see her, to see all of her, drives me as my hands map the shape of her waist, over her hips, slipping under her shirt to pull it off. With tantalizing slowness, I reveal her to my hot stare for the first time. My calloused hands a rough contrast over the silkiness of her flesh.

Color me surprised when the move reveals a black lace bra, her perfect tits testing the confines of the sexy material. My hands unconsciously move to the lace like a heat seeking missile, tugging the cups down to prop up her swollen flesh, the black lace a beautiful contrast to her pale skin.

This is a sight that will be burned in my memory for the rest of my life. My imagination just does not do her justice.

I've spent hours fantasizing about the body she hides behind her conservative clothes. Some men would overlook her, mistakenly assume the body underneath is nothing special. The shy exterior hiding the passion within.

My eyes eat up the perfection in front of me. The swell of her tits, tipped with dusky rose nipples just begging for my mouth. The deceptive fullness – I know will overflow my hands – tapering down to a narrow waist I could wrap my hands around before flaring into shapely hips.

My mind blanks, my focus solely on the beauty before me, breath expelling from my lungs in a rush.

I must have been admiring the erotic picture too long, lost in the fantasies swirling in my head. In a self-conscious move, her hands come up in an attempt to cover herself.

I catch them in a firm grip. "Don't hide yourself. You're beautiful."

The blush that so fascinates me starts at the tops of those beautiful tits. I watch it travel up her chest and over her neck before settling in her cheeks.

Her eagerness is irresistible as she awaits my next move.

Taking her hands, I use my own to squeeze them around her tits. Pressing together so both her nipples are close enough for me to play with.

Glancing up to capture her gaze, I warn. "Keep your hands right there. Don't move until I tell you to. If you move, I stop."

My commanding tone gets her hot. The clench of thighs gives her away. Confident she'll follow direction, I flick my tongue out to tease first one nipple then the other before zeroing in with teasing licks of her areola and sharp bites to the tip.

Her heaving breaths force the soft flesh further into my mouth. Arousal shoots down my spine as the expelled air brushes across my face from where she watches me devour her.

I continue the torture of her other bud, captured between my fingers. Her responsiveness is a thing of beauty driving my desire higher. I'm dangerously close to exploding and we're just getting started.

Kissing across the stunning cleavage created by her tight hold, I give my attention to her neglected nipple. Treating it to the same licks and nips, my tongue swirls around the hard nub.

I take advantage of her attention riveted to the play of my tongue to unbutton her jeans. She is so lost in the moment, I slide them over her hips without protest.

Her soft skin is perfection. My hands itch to touch what my eyes are devouring. The cold air in the room caresses over her revealed skin, raising goosebumps in its wake.

Leaving the material of her jeans at her knees, I trail my fingers back up her shapely thighs. The rough pads a contrast as I trace up her slim thighs to the treasure hidden from my view. Black lace conceals the pussy I'm dying to get my mouth on.

Looking up, I devour the sight of my ultimate fantasy still offering her tits to me.

"Is my Siren wet?" I can't resist teasing her more, testing how far I can push her. The blush spreads so prettily up her chest even as she nods eagerly.

Quicksilver flows through my blood, lighting a fire in my blood at the vision of her completely caught up in the moment.

At knowing I accomplished that.

"Put your hand in your panties and show me." Without hesitation, she releases her soft flesh with one hand to trail down the smooth skin of her stomach.

She follows my directions beautifully. Her shyness a thing of the past, lost to the power of her arousal.

Pride swells as I watch her overcome the ingrained emotions as she gets lost in the eroticism of our play.

The hidden temptress with the wild curls and sinful body, has fully emerged in front of me.

She's the forbidden Siren calling me to my demise.

I'd willingly follow her to my death for the chance at the promise land between her thighs. My dick weeps at the thought of that sweet little pussy wrapped around it.

I can't resist another test of her inhibitions. "Tease your nipple with your other hand. The same way I did."

Her hand moves before I even finish my command, fingers squeeze her nipple even as her right hand starts its descent. Reaching the lace hiding her pussy, her hand continues inside the sexy black lace shielding her movements from my view.

My imagination doesn't compare to the eroticism of her overcoming her inhibitions.

My dick strains to escape the confines of my jeans as her panties shift, her fingers playing. The sight of her lost in her pleasure increases my own desire.

I didn't believe it was possible to get any harder.

I was wrong.

Precum leaks from the tip, escaping to soak my boxer briefs. Thankfully, the wet spot hides behind my jeans.

For a man who normally lasts for hours, the sight of that wetness would be an embarrassment, a testament to how close to the edge I really am. And the power she holds over me.

"Sink two fingers in your pussy. Get them nice and wet for me." Her eyes close at my newest command.

Goosebumps pop up under my hands still gripping her hips. A sure sign she enjoys following my lead.

But I need to see her, see the desire her eyes can't hide. "Open your eyes."

She follows my command at the same time her hand emerges from her panties, fingers glistening with her arousal.

Mouth salivating, I lean forward to suck those fingers into my mouth before her hand even stops moving.

I'm addicted with just one taste of the sweetness bursting on my tongue.

My fingers curl impatiently into the lace at her hips, using my hold to yank her on the bed with me while at the same time stripping her of the lace. I flip her to her back, settling into the cradle of her thighs.

My nip at her lips until they part on a moan. Taking full advantage, I slip my tongue inside to explore her mouth in a filthy caress. The thrust of my tongue an imitation of the way my dick will soon be ravaging her.

I slip my hand to the heaven between her legs, my fingers gliding through the wetness pooling there.

She wasn't lying. She is soaked.

Reluctantly I disentangle myself, standing impatient to remove my clothes. Dying for the feel of her without the barrier of my clothes, pulling a condom from my wallet before I carelessly toss that too.

As I straighten to my full height, she gets her first look at my dick, my hand strangling the base to hold off my orgasm.

It's not even funny how close I am to blowing my load.

This is a new experience for me. With other women, I could fuck for hours.

There is just something about Kate that tests my control.

Her whispered "wow" certainly isn't helping my situation.

Dropping back down to the bed, I hover over her petite body, coming to a stop on my hands and knees so I don't crush her with my weight.

"You want this, Siren?" I ask.

Her nod is instantaneous but I need more.

"Say it." I can't help but push her. I need the words.

There's a short hesitation but then she gives me the words I crave. "Yes Mac. I want this. I want you."

Thank fuck.

Chapter Seventeen

Kate

Mac is the vision of a sexual conqueror hovering above me. His hardness fills my vision where it stands proudly in front of me. All my senses are fully engaged, overloaded, as I watch the slide of the condom down his thick length. Just a hint of trepidation lingers.

He's huge. Much larger than my previous sexual partner.

Nerves try to push in even as I get ensnared in his predatory gaze. His sensual spell was obviously meant to heighten my desire to the point of no return before revealing his size.

The fact that this man has worked so hard to ensure my comfort does more to relax me than anything else.

I'm all in this with him.

"Ready?" He's sweet to check.

In answer, I slide my hands around his neck, pulling him down for another kiss, affirming my full participation. He wastes no time returning his focus to my aching core.

As I get lost in his soul stealing kiss, the swirling tip of his finger teases through my wetness before moving down to circle my entrance. A wave of pleasure brings with it an involuntary clench as he breaches my core.

"Relax." He commands. "I don't want to hurt you."

"Easy for you to say." But I follow his order, doing my best to relax my muscles – rewarded with another wave of awe inspiring pleasure when he sinks into the depths of my core, the fullness of his thick fingers pumping in and out slowly.

As if my senses weren't already overloaded, he adds to my intoxication, his lips leave a fiery trail along my breasts.

"Mac." His name is nothing more than a sigh from my lips.

My mind can't decide which sensations to focus on. As caught up in him as I am, I recognize that's exactly what he wants. And then all thoughts flee.

I let my mind go and surrender to his spell as he builds my arousal higher and higher. Just as my body is teetering on the precipice, he adds yet another layer. In a swift move, he lowers his large body down until all I can see is his dark hair between my thighs.

Oh, but I feel.

That talented mouth latches onto my clit, strong pulls join the harsh thrust of his fingers.

He plays my body like a maestro. I am completely at his mercy as an orgasm detonates through me. Never before have I felt such pleasure.

He's taken me so far beyond any peak before him.

It's a joke to even call them sexual encounters and he's not even inside me yet.

Mac crawls up my body while I lay here, muscles drained, caught up in the sensual fog he so expertly weaves. Towering over my body like a predator, his hardness notches at my opening, already reigniting my desire.

He breaches my entrance, with gently yet firmly, the perfect combination of pressure. Slow and steady, he rocks back and forth, stretching my internal muscles to accommodate his size. The stretch is a burn in the best possible way. His fingers were no match for the fullness of him completely entrenched in my core.

Curses fly past his lips when my core clenches uncontrollably. "Don't do that. I'm holding on by a thread. Your pussy is strangling my dick."

It's laughable he thinks that would help. His words have the exact opposite effect. I can't control the rhythmic squeezing any more than I could resist his sensual spell.

I can do nothing but stare up at him in pleasurable wonder. "I'm sorry, I can't help it. You feel so good."

The wonder in my voice echoes the amazement of my thoughts.

My words snap his control. Mac pulls almost all the way out before thrusting back in. Hard.

All before I even finish speaking.

Back and forth, over and over, he owns me. Reading the signs of my body to guide his movements.

Reading the pleasure on my face to bring me to another surprising precipice.

Taking no pity on my overwhelmed body, he doubles down to push me over the building peak.

My mind blanks.

Fireworks explode behind my eyes.

And I'm soaring.

His name is a plea screaming past my lips.

No embarrassment at how loud I am.

No concern that anyone could hear me.

Just Mac and me. Soaring through the stars.

My name escapes as a groan as he follows me over. I watch in wonder at the pleasure playing out across his face.

Arms giving out, his weight cocoons me as his large body engulfs mine. A feeling of protectiveness washes through more than my body.

My heart feels it too.

Stop Kate. It's just sex, really, really good sex, but just sex.

After a last lingering kiss, he rolls away to get rid of the condom before returning to the bed. He pulls me right back into his arms like he can't stand the thought of any distance separating us.

With a tender press of his lips to my shoulder, he pulls me in close to his chest, holding tight like he'll never let go.

"Get some rest. We are definitely gonna be doing that again soon."

I sigh in contentment and burrow into the security of his embrace.

Unable to fight the call of slumber, I'm asleep soon after.

True to his word, Mac wakes me twice more during the night, ravishing my body to wring even more orgasms from me.

We talk between bouts of sex, opening up to each other in a way I never have. I share pieces of myself I've never shared with anyone.

We finally drift off as the first morning rays of light filter through the window.

I'm surprised at how easily Mac breached my defenses when I've never gone that deep with any other man.

I just hope he's worth it.

Chapter Eighteen

Mac

The first rays of sunlight shining through the window jolts me from the most peaceful sleep I've had in years, the perfection of Kate wrapped in my arms. I do nothing to fight the urge to bury my face in the riot of wild curls, captivated by her alluring scent. An intoxicating mixture bringing to mind an orange grove lit by clear blue skies.

I slide out of bed carefully so as not to wake her. Bending to pick up my jeans, I quietly slide them on, leaving the button undone as I pull on a clean shirt.

I let my eyes run over the captivating beauty asleep in my bed. Masculine satisfaction fills me as she continues to sleep so peacefully.

The beast inside roaring, I did that to her. Took her to unparalleled heights of pleasure. The explosion of which surprised even me. I knew we would be explosive together but damn.

She needs her rest after our long night. Regretfully, I leave her to rest, silently closing the door behind me.

I'm overdue for a check in with Byte so I head to his room first, not surprised in the slightest to find him in his usual spot in front of the lit monitors. His fingers fly over his keyboard.

A smirk spreads over the assholes face when he sees me. "Hey man. Didn't think you'd be up this early."

It's no secret I never sleep in. Even last night's sex marathon with Kate didn't change that.

Ignoring his knowing look, I get right to it, anxious to return to the beauty in my bed. "What happened with the trucker?"

"He wasn't home when Bomber and Joker went to visit. The wife was there with two kids but she didn't have much to say. Bomb thinks she is hiding something but Joker thinks she's just scared."

Interesting that they had such different opinions on the wife.

"What do you think?" Byte wasn't only our tech expert. His instincts about people are eerily accurate.

He's the best judge of character I've ever met.

"Not sure yet. I think we should pay her a visit too." He says.

"Do you think that's a good idea when the club was just there?" I worry we'll tip our hand or force the wife into hiding. We were intimidating as fuck.

If the trucker really is involved in the drugs running through town, I don't want to send our only link to him into hiding too.

Byte and I have gone through his life with a fine tooth comb. Other than the trips out of state, he hasn't been seen around Frostown or anywhere near his house.

"From what Joker said, the asshole hasn't been home in weeks. The wife said he's been on a long haul run but bank records don't support that." He says before continuing. "Financials show he has a room at the Future Casino in Mississippi but no one has set eyes on him there."

"Well then, I guess we really don't have much of a choice. Let's head over there this afternoon." I agree. "What about the teacher?"

"Nothing on him yet. So far, he's coming back squeaky clean." I feel his frustration. There usually isn't anyone Byte can't easily find.

We need to find something more than the cousin's connection to the school. If there is something there, I have no doubt Byte will find it. A dog with a bone has nothing on Byte when he has someone in his crosshairs.

With nothing else to do until we head to the truckers house, I leave him to his work.

Not that he notices. He goes right back to whatever is on his monitors.

I run into Ryker outside Byte's room, and together we cross the main room to the kitchen.

I need an infusion of caffeine stat.

I catch him up on my plans with Byte. "Byte thinks we should visit the trucker's house again. Even if he's not home, he thinks we can get something from the wife."

Ear hustler that he is, Joker shows no shame in chiming in. "You're going back to the trucker's house?"

"Yeah. This afternoon." I say.

"I think I'll go with." There's a new glint in his eyes this morning. His easygoing demeanor nowhere in sight.

"Okay. Byte is working on something. We'll head out in a few hours." I tell him.

In a flash, his normal humor returns as he takes a jab at the brother not there to defend himself. "Probably getting his daily dose of porn. His dick is gonna fall off with all the jerking he does."

As usual, a slap to the back of his head is Ryker's only response. Prez doesn't need to say anything.

Brother is never gonna learn when to keep his mouth shut.

I take that as my cue to get lost. My long strides carry me back to my room – more importantly to the beauty recuperating in my bed.

Silently entering the room, I eagerly drop my clothes then slide back in the bed behind her, happy to see she's in the exact spot I left her. I simply watch her for several long moments, taking in the way she looks in my bed.

So good, I don't ever want to let her out of it.

Even in sleep, her body seeks me out as her ass snuggles right up to my hardening dick. My hand has a mind of its own, mapping over her waist, gliding down all that soft skin to cup her pussy.

Her lips spread as my fingers circle, not quite making contact with her clit. Instead, slowly teasing up and down, my aim to stir her desire high enough to wake her.

Her hips swivel, pushing her delectable ass even harder into the cradle of my hips.

When a moan escapes her lips, I lean forward to whisper in her ear. "Good morning, Siren."

Her grumbled "good morning" is amusing. She's adorably grouchy this morning. But she can't hide her body's response. Her opening pulses against my fingers, wetness escaping to aid my tease.

Satisfied that she's ready for me, I pull away only far enough to grab a condom then lift her leg over mine, spreading her wide open.

"I love how wet you get for me, Siren. Your pussy sucks me in so greedy. So tight, so wet. Gonna fuck you until it's all you think about. All consuming." The words grind out.

Her cream soaks me even more, paves the way for my entry through swollen flesh until my hips are once again pressed flush to her ass, this time my dick fully entrenched in her wet heat.

What I wouldn't give to feel her without a barrier between us.

The visual ramps my desire and my fingers grip her inner thigh tighter, lifting to make more room for my lazy thrusts, her body at my mercy.

This angle allows for deeper penetration. I'm hitting her g-spot. Her pussy clenches on my dick as more cream escapes.

"You're close, aren't you baby?" Her moan an affirmative, her pussy gripping impossibly tighter, strangling my dick.

Slowly, oh so slowly, I tease her orgasm to the surface. Maintaining a maddeningly slow pace.

"Mac." Her breathing accelerates, her climax gaining speed. Gasping moans pour from her chest as she flies higher. "So close. Feels so good."

"That's right. Squeeze my dick. Show me who owns it."

Drifting my hand down her stomach, I find her clit, squeezing it between two fingers. Giving her the pressure to push her over the edge, the orgasm pulsing through her body, her internal muscles strangling my dick.

Shifting our position, I roll her fully under my body until she's pressed flat to the mattress. I pull back far enough to lift her ass to the angle I want, allowing me to go even deeper.

I last through only a few more thrusts into heaven before my orgasm hits, triggering another from her that takes us both by surprise.

At the last second, enough brain cells return to roll my boneless body to the side to avoid crushing her with my dead weight.

I trail lingering kisses over her shoulder as my heart rate returns to normal.

"I don't want to leave this bed." Her back arches in a sensuous stretch I feel through my entire body.

"Hmm. I think you have the right idea." She purrs.

Disappointment surges. I hate to break the bubble we've wrapped ourselves in since last night. "I wish we could stay here all day. I'm just getting started with you."

"But you can't?" The pout in her voice lights a smile on my face.

At least I'm not alone in my disappointment.

"No, baby. I need to do some things for the club today."

Her sigh sets guilt stirring inside me. "That's okay. I need to check in on April anyway."

With a last lingering kiss, I pull away to get dressed so I can take her home.

Luckily, we escape the clubhouse without running into any of my brothers. No doubt, they heard us last night. Pride explodes, even knowing how embarrassed she would be at the thought of anyone hearing us.

The ride to her house perfect with her body wrapped tight around me. I leave her with a heated kiss at her door.

It takes all my self-control to walk away without her.

Chapter Nineteen

Kate

My usual greeting spills from my lips as I walk through the front door. "Honey, I'm home!"

Not really expecting it, I'm surprised to see April up and in the kitchen. Usually, it takes a herculean effort to drag her out of bed before noon on the weekends. It's then I realize she has been up early a lot lately. Not sure what's up with that. "Did you finish your paper?" I ask.

"Yes, I finished most of it this morning, just putting the finishing touches on it now." She says.

I worry about April.

Aside from Aaron, she doesn't have any friends. I don't want her to miss out on the unique experiences of her senior year like I did. She should be out having fun with her friends and classmates.

"Why don't you call Aaron and get out to do something fun?" I suggest.

"I don't know." She's obvious in her hesitation.

"Come on, April. You should be out having fun! It's your last year of high school. Your last chance to be carefree before life becomes real."

"You're always trying to force me to do things I don't want to do." The hurt look crossing her face slices right through me.

Stunned by her reaction, I backpedal in an attempt to calm her down. "April, honey, I just think you should be going out and having fun. I don't want you to have the same regrets I did."

"I'm not you, Kate." She says bitterly. "You go out almost every night now, and that's not something I want or need to do."

Shock and hurt collide, I can do nothing but watch as she storms out of the kitchen, no idea where all this is coming from.

At a loss, I ponder what to do with myself. There is no way I can focus on planning for the upcoming week right now.

A glance at the clock shows Sweet Treats is still open.

I should be able to catch Demi before she closes.

She's always a good distraction.

As I rush through my shower, I decide to leave a note for April to let her know where I'm going. To text me if she wants anything from the bakery.

Hopefully she takes the olive branch.

It is a beautiful day, deciding a walk will do me good. I end up practically skipping down the street in anticipation of seeing my friend.

My feet grind to a stop as I turn the corner, the bakery full to bursting. My heart warms for my friend, the reality of the fulfillment of her dream right there in front of me.

The whirlwind that is Demi swirls behind the counter when I enter the bakery. All the tables are full, even more people wait outside the door.

Making a split-second decision, I quickly slide behind the counter.

My friend needs some help.

"You're a lifesaver. I don't know where this crowd came from but I'm not looking a gift horse in the mouth!" There's relief in her words even with her usual sarcasm trying to mask it.

The next hour flies by as we take care of her customers.

It takes only a few minutes to get the hang of the cash register. After that, we get into a groove like we've been doing this for years.

By the time the last customer is served, it's time for Demi to close up shop for the day.

I chat with Rebecca Dawson while boxing up her muffin. "How's your aunt doing? She hasn't called me for anything lately."

I helped Rebecca's aunt after a knee replacement last year. I stopped by at least twice a week after her surgery. Even though she has family, I was happy to help in any way I could. Most of our time spent catching her up on any juicy gossip she was missing.

I miss her.

"She's doing good. The doctor cleared her medical release last month. She's been making up for lost time gossiping down at the diner." She says with a laugh.

Sounds like nothing's changed there.

"I'm so glad she's doing well. I miss spending time with her." I have fond memories of our time together.

"You should stop by. I'm sure she would love to see you."

I agree with a smile as I ring her up and finally move to join Demi at our table.

My feet sigh in relief when I drop into my seat. I take a sip of the mouthwatering coffee as we relax in the eerily quiet bakery.

My friend doesn't let that last long. I think she's incapable of just appreciating the peace in the silence.

"So, Kate. What did you do last night?" She doesn't give me a chance to respond. "I was surprised when I didn't hear from you."

If there's one thing I can count on, it's that my new friend has no qualms about jumping right in on the inquisition.

Attempting avoidance, I go with a vague response. "It was good."

And I would have gotten away with it if the blush creeping up my neck didn't sell me out.

"Hmm, I'm not buying that." She disagrees. "A little birdie told me you spent the night at the clubhouse with Mac."

Well shoot. How could she possibly know that?

Not ready to give in just yet, I try diversion this time. "Sounds like you may know more than me. Who's the little birdie?"

Waving my question away, her grin turns downright devious. "No one important. Tell me. Did Mac live up to your fantasies?"

My cheeks are on fire now. There's no way she'll let me distract her this time.

Knowing when I'm beat, I tell her about Mac's visit to my house yesterday.

And his explanation about what she saw with Josie.

She doesn't seem to buy his recounting of the scene she walked in on but for once keeps her thoughts on that to herself.

I catch her up on the rest of my night. Not all the juicy details because she just doesn't need to know how far he pushed me out of my comfort zone.

I wouldn't even know how to start with that.

"Whew, I knew he would rock your world." She's true to form in her outrageousness even as she fans herself.

Her smirk at the giggle I couldn't contain if my life depended on it, is that of the Cheshire cat. It lasts mere seconds before she takes on a serious expression. "Just be careful. I don't want to see you hurt. I can already see you're into him." Her hand squeezes my own to soften her warning but it doesn't stop the doubt swarming in my belly.

What she says is true.

I *am* into him. More so than any man before him. I need to guard my heart or he'll have the power to shred it to pieces if he betrays me.

Covering my disquiet with another smile, I change the focus back to her. "So business is good. I think you need to hire someone. At least part time help would be better than nothing." I suggest.

That's enough doom and gloom for today.

Silently acknowledging my need to take the spotlight off myself, she gives me the out.

At least for now.

"You may be right. I've been so preoccupied setting up the bakery and building a clientele the past few months, I didn't realize how much this place consumes my entire life." Her words are wistful. "But really what do I have to complain about? I made my dream a reality and it's prospering faster than I thought possible."

"Maybe put out a help wanted sign?" I suggest. "See what kind of interest you get."

"Yeah, I think you're right. I'll work on it tomorrow." She concedes.

Taking my last sip of caffeinated yumminess, I run out of excuses to avoid going home. "Okay. I guess I should get home. I'll talk to you later."

Too slow to dodge her, Demi wraps me in the bear hug I managed to avoid earlier before I head out the door, the chime of the old fashioned bell announcing my departure.

With radio silence from April, I take a leisurely stroll home, checking out the storefront windows of the shops on Main Street. It won't be long until the leaves are changing and cooler mornings driving out the heat of this sweltering summer.

April's door is still closed when I return home so I decide the best thing to do is give her some space.

Sitting down at the kitchen table, I'm finally able to focus on planning my lessons for the week. And more importantly, where to fit in my volunteer hours.

Chapter Twenty

Mac

Joker, Byte and I pull up in front of a dilapidated house in a shitty neighborhood in Redford, the silence deafening when our engines shut off after the hour-long drive to the trucker's house.

My blood boils as I take in the state of the house. The out-of-control yard. The crumbling front porch. Weeds explode through the cracks of the sidewalk underfoot as we make our way to the door.

"Man. This is worse than you described." Byte's comment is directed at Joker. "I don't think that porch is going to hold all our weight."

Ignoring him, Joker moves up the steps. "You guys wait here. I don't want to scare the wife. She was skittish last time we were here. Maybe she'll be more comfortable if she sees a familiar face."

I share a concerned look with Byte behind Joker's back. We're thinking the same thing.

His interest in the married woman is an issue.

Joker may be a lot of things but a home wrecker is not one of them. He comes from a broken home himself – his dad constantly cheated on his mom.

Joker is vocal about his strong feelings on adultery.

We wait for the door to open after the bang of his fist, the wood just about splintering from the force. The only movement from inside is the shift of a curtain in the narrow window beside the door.

Joker bangs his fist against the wood again. "Sarah, we know you're in there. We're not here to hurt you. We just want to talk to Vinny."

His words must have been the assurance she needed. The door swings open, exposing a petite blond about twenty pounds underweight.

She's swimming in her clothes. Skin and bones from the looks of it, like she hasn't eaten in weeks.

Her downcast eyes complete the picture of meekness. She is obviously hanging on by a thread, battered down to this submissive version that pisses me off. DeLuca isn't a man.

He's a bastard for leaving his family in this shitty situation.

"I told you the last time you were here, he hasn't been home. He's on a long haul to California." She says.

"Sarah, we know he's not on the road. He hasn't been on a run for months." Joker breaks the news to her.

"What?" An actress she is not. There is no way to hide her surprise at Joker's revelation.

Ignoring her question, Joker gently presses her for information. "Is there anyone that he's close to? Anywhere you can think of he would go to hide?"

"The only family he has is a cousin that works at the high school in Frostown. Michael Smith." That isn't new intel for us.

"We already checked him out. He's not there." Byte raises his voice to join the conversation from where we hang back several feet away. Joker was right to stop us from approaching the house with him.

"Then I don't know where he is. Apparently, there's a lot I don't know." My anger reaches a boiling point at the defeat in her voice.

Her douchebag husband threw her under the bus without a care. Leaving her to deal with mounting debt. Strangers showing up at her door. On top of taking care of his kids.

"Do you have anywhere you can go? Any family that can help you?" Joker changes tactics, pulling her attention back to him. "We're far from the worst of visitors that will come looking for him."

All color drains from her face as she shakes her head. "No, my parents passed before my oldest was born and I don't have any other family."

Her shitty situation becomes starkly clear the more she talks. She's not staying out of loyalty to the bastard. She's stuck here.

"Will you at least take my number?" Joker presses. "We can help if you'll let us." I see the indecision in her expression, she doesn't understand yet that she can trust us.

"Think about your kids, Sarah. You don't want your husband to bring some bad shit down on them." Joker's words finally convince her to take the offer.

Silently, she hands him her phone, waiting patiently for him to enter his number. He listens for the ring of his own phone before handing it back to her. "Call day or night, if you need anything."

Not releasing the phone, he presses when she says nothing, her eyes gravitating back down to the ground. "I mean it, Sarah. Day or night, I'll be here."

We watch as she takes the phone before closing the door softly. The lock turns seconds later.

Only then does Joker retrace his steps down the dilapidated porch. Ignoring us, he doesn't wait as he mounts his bike and roars off down the street.

"I'm worried about him." Byte voices the concerns running through my mind. Joker comes across as a man with no worries but it's all a front.

While the brothers know some of his background, we all inherently understand it is much darker than any of us are aware of.

"Come on. There's nothing we can do about it right now. Let's head back to the clubhouse." I say.

We mount up and follow Joker's lead out of the shitty neighborhood for the long drive back to Frostown.

Chapter Twenty-One

Kate

Wednesday afternoon finds me sitting in my usual spot in the staff break room, munching on the salad I don't really want. The crunch of the fresh leaves no match for the gooey chocolate that oozes from the fresh flakiness of one of Demi's sinful croissants.

Demi has spoiled me with her baked yumminess. To the point I seriously need to increase my workouts if I want to continue fitting into my pants. And eat this sad salad.

At the moment, I can't really find it in myself to care when I choke down another bite of my boring lunch.

If the tradeoff is sinful yumminess, maybe a size up isn't a bad thing.

A few of my coworkers chat as they lounge around the break room. With my table of one, you can see I'm not the most social person.

Some things never change. It's like high school all over again.

Loneliness doesn't hit me like it normally would. I probably have Mac and Demi to thank for that.

No sooner does the thought cross my mind, I catch sight of Michael Smith sauntering over before he drops down in the chair across from me.

"Hi. Kate, right?" While his attention is somewhat expected, I am surprised he approached me at the school. He's never deigned to speak to me before.

"Hello. Yep, that's me."

I'm not sure what's more surprising – the handsome teacher coming to talk to me or my lack of shyness in the face of casual conversation.

Not that I am a generally chatty person but I'm not usually one to easily engage in normal chit chat.

"I don't think we've formally met. I'm Michael Smith. I have the American History class down the hall from you."

Nodding, I don't really feel the need to respond. He's not telling me anything I don't already know. More than anything, I'm curious why he chose now to approach me.

I'm almost a hundred percent sure it has something to do with the club's investigation.

He doesn't leave me hanging for long. "I hear you volunteer with the seniors and disabled in town. Assisting with errands and shopping they are no longer able to do on their own?"

"Yes, that's right. I try to help wherever I can. It's something I hope someone would do for me if I needed it." I admit.

A smarmy smile crosses his face. "Do you think you'd have time to add another? My Aunt Ginny has a bad hip and isn't able to get out much. I'm so busy with the football team now. Coaching during the season, conditioning during the off-season. I don't have as much time as I would like to help her."

He sure jumped right to the point.

I can use this to my advantage. If I get close to his aunt, maybe I can find out if he truly is involved with the drug dealing in town. Mac definitely won't like it but I'll deal with that later.

He'll be fine. If I can get information for the club, it will be worth it.

"Sure, I'd be happy to help her." I agree quickly. Positive I can learn something useful for the club.

"Great, she'll be excited. Like I said, she doesn't get out much anymore and I'm sure she'll love you. This will really help me out. I feel guilty that I haven't had much time for her lately."

Not sure why he's telling me all this.

Not wanting to be rude – the excuses are familiar – I keep my response neutral. "Well, I'll make sure I plan my schedule to spend some time with her. I know what it's like to be lonely."

Way to sound pathetic Kate. Now he's going to think you're fishing for company.

Embarrassed, I continue quickly to cover my asinine commentary. "Does she know you're arranging a volunteer for her?"

"Yes. I didn't think you'd say no. Everyone said you didn't have it in you to refuse." He smirks overconfidently.

Gross, he's got an ego to rival a few of Mac's brother's.

The question is, why is he pulling out the charm if he was so confident I would agree?

I keep those uncharitable thoughts to myself as I search my purse for my notebook. This thing is the only way I could possibly keep my life in order.

I hand it over for him to add her information.

The better to get me out of this awkward exchange faster.

This guy is putting off some seriously creepy vibes.

When he hands the notebook back to me, I tuck it away, standing to clean up my unappetizing lunch.

"Can I get your number to give my aunt so she, has it?" For some reason his seemingly innocent question gives me pause.

"Um, I'll just text her first, so she knows who's calling when I have my schedule set." I avoid.

Mac already won't be happy that I agreed to this without talking to him first. No need to add to his displeasure by handing out my number.

"Okay." By the tightening around his smile, it's clear he doesn't care for my avoidance. "I'll let her know to expect your text."

Welcome to the club, douche. I don't care for you either.

Assured I made the right call, I check the time. The hands of the clock a sign I'm going to be late getting back to my classroom if I don't get moving.

I break eye contact and gather my sorry lunch.

Ugh gross, it gets more disgusting the longer it sits out.

I toss the unappetizing thing in the trash on my way out the door.

"Have a good rest of your day." I quickly exit the break room, not really caring if he responds.

Chapter Twenty-Two

Mac

Kate and I haven't been able to connect since the night she rocked my world. Random texts about the only way she's communicating this week.

If she wasn't fully engaged in our exchanges, I'd be worried my intensity scared her off.

The sound of my phone draws my eyes for the millionth time.

Speak of the devil.

I don't even try to hold back my smile when her name flashes up on my screen.

It is completely uncontrollable. I feel zero shame about it.

She must sense she's on my mind.

Siren: Hey I only have a few minutes tonight. I have a new client I need to introduce myself to but I need to talk to you first.

Me: Everything ok? I thought we could take a ride again

Way to sound pathetic asshole.

Not gonna lie. Her canceling on me *again* is depressing.

We've been playing this game all week.

Even though I know volunteering is her passion, there is no controlling this insane desire to have her all to myself.

I don't care if that makes me an asshole. She makes me want to force my way into her life. To bask in her bright light, that inner beauty that others overlook.

Siren: Sorry it's a new client and I'm not sure how long I'll be there. According to her nephew she's lonely so I want to spend some time getting to know her.

Me: You don't know her? How did you get connected with her?

Siren: This is why I want to talk to you. I'm on my way there now.

No more than five minutes pass before she bounds through the clubhouse doors. I'm not the only man riveted by the sway of her sexy ass walking my way. It's almost enough to distract me from my distress at her urgency to see me.

Almost.

"Siren." I'm off my stool and moving to meet her before I even know it.

Wrapping her in my arms, I pull her close to bury my face in the sweet sensitive spot of her neck that drives her wild. The fresh clean scent that is all Kate engulfs my senses as she slips her arms around my neck.

"Who's the nephew?" I don't let her distract me from the burning need to know.

"It's Michael Smith." Confirmation that it is the connection to DeLuca freezes the blood in my veins. My arms tighten around her unconsciously.

"Absolutely not." I bark out.

She keeps going, ignoring me. "He said she has problems with her hip and isn't able to get out anymore. I want to see if I can find anything out from her. But more than anything, I want to help if she truly needs it."

Equal parts fear and foreboding unfurl in my chest, a lethal combination threatening to bring me to my knees. The connection between the teacher and DeLuca too coincidental not to mean something.

"Kate, you can't do this. It's too dangerous." My words grind out.

"We don't know that. He might not even be involved." She argues. "This is a chance to find out. I'll be fine. You won't let anything bad happen to me."

Her faith in me is misplaced. I'm not the hero she believes I am.

"I need to talk to Byte. Come on." Clutching her hand in a firm grip, I lead her to my room.

"Stay here." Leaving her there, I tear through the clubhouse in search of Byte, irrationally panicked our second visit to DeLuca's tipped our hand.

"Byte!" My voice booms through the clubhouse when there's no sign of him.

What feels like an eternity later, he strolls out of the kitchen with Ryker.

"What's up, brother?" It's Ryker that asks.

"We fucked up, man. Smith is sniffing around Kate. He set her up to meet with his aunt." Finger quotes accompany the word aunt. I have no idea if he even has an aunt.

"Byte, get back to it. Find out if he has an aunt and what condition she's in." Ever the voice of reason – no matter the situation – Ryker calmly issues his orders.

This is the reason he's our Prez. The reason we all respect his leadership. He takes control with an enviable calmness driven by analytical thinking and logic. He never lets emotions rule him.

His hand on my shoulder breaks through my emotional upheaval. I'm so caught up in it, I didn't even notice his approach. "You need to calm down, man. We gotta think rationally. There's no evidence they know we're onto them."

I am about as far from calm as a person can be, it would be laughable if it wasn't my woman on the line here. Fear is a paralysis that's fucking with my mind right now.

His slap on my back snaps me out of it again. "Come on. I can see you're not going to calm down until we know more. Let's go see what Byte has."

Moving swiftly down the hallway, we enter Byte's room to see his eyes are all for his monitors.

"The aunt checks out. Ginny Smith. Sixty-six years old. Homebound with a bad hip. She hasn't recovered well from a surgery last year. From what I can see, she doesn't get many visitors. The nephew's visits dropped off several weeks ago." He doesn't look away from his screen.

"Doesn't mean he's not using her as bait. They could be onto us after our visits to DeLuca's." I'm not ready to believe it's all an innocent coincidence.

"We'll put a brother on your woman when she goes there." Ryker promises. "Keep watch over her in case they try to pull something."

"She's here. Let me go grab her so we can talk." While not the perfect solution, I grudgingly agree.

The only thing that would completely put me at ease is keeping Kate as far from that asshole as possible.

The instinct to protect her at all costs wars with the faith I normally have in Prez's leadership.

Stopping in the hallway, back pressed to the wall, I take a deep breath, struggling to get myself under control.

When the vise in my chest loosens, I hustle to my room for Kate.

"Come on, babe. Let's go talk to Ryker."

I wrap my hand around hers, threading our fingers to lock down the beast roaring to break free at the thought of anything happening to her.

Ryker and Byte wait for us at the bar when we re-enter the main room.

"Hey guys." She throws them a nervous wave.

"Kate, we confirmed that Smith does in fact have an aunt that needs help. Doesn't mean that he's not using her as bait to get close to you." Not wasting time on pleasantries, Ryker jumps right into it.

She's nodding halfway through his explanation. "I understand that. I want to help and I think this will be the perfect way to do that."

"Siren, you don't have to do this. The club is following leads on both Smith and his cousin." I say in the hope she'll change her mind.

I should have known better.

"Mac, I want to help. I need to know the drug dealing is going to stop." Her hand cups my cheek to soften the blow of her persistence.

Her words do the opposite, igniting anger as I pull back from her touch.

"Kate, don't do this." Putting herself in danger is unacceptable. Not when I don't trust that I'll be able to protect her.

"You can't do this. I won't allow it." Unable to voice my true fears, I lash out instead.

Head rearing back, the shock on her face wars with anger.

"You don't get to make that decision." She lets me have it. "Mac, don't you see? I need to help but I will be smart about it."

Dismissing me for the moment, she turns back to Ryker. "Do you have a plan?"

"Yes. We'll keep a man on you during your visits. If anything happens, someone will be there to have your back." He assures her.

"Thank you, Ryker. Will you please give me a few minutes with Mac?" She turns her back to them, dismissing them before he even agrees.

He steps up next to me. "Brother, you gotta trust that we got this. Your girl is smart. She won't put herself in unnecessary danger." With that parting shot, he follows Byte to the back of the clubhouse.

Once they're out of the room, Kate turns to me with a soft smile, her anger gone.

"Mac, I need to do this. I couldn't live with myself if I didn't." She says

Bringing my hands up to cup her face, my fingers caress the soft skin of her cheeks as I force myself to voice my greatest fear. "Baby, I wouldn't be able to live with myself if something happens to you."

"Nothing is going to happen to me, Mac. I trust in you and your friends. I know you'll keep me safe." Her words tame the beast inside just enough to allow a little bit of logic to return. "Mac, I couldn't live with myself if someone else gets hurt and there was something I could have done to help."

"But what if something happens to you? You think I could live with knowing you put yourself in danger to help us?" I'm not ready to give up.

"I'll be careful Mac, but I need to do this." Her hands caress down my sides. The muscles of my abdomen expanding as she uses her hold to pull me closer, wrapping herself around me.

"I don't want anything to happen to you." I'm fighting a losing battle. It's there in her eyes.

"Mac, I have faith that you will protect me."

What she doesn't understand is I don't deserve her faith in me.

"What if I don't have the same faith in myself?" The question is nothing more than a brush of air over her curls where I've buried my face.

"Then I'll just have to have enough faith for both of us." Conviction rings in her voice.

Instead of packing her away to keep her from getting so much as a paper cut, I try to trust in Prez's instincts. In Kate's assurance.

"Okay, baby. I'll give you this for now but at the first sign of anything shady, I'm pulling you out fast. You stay safe and call me when you get home tonight or if anything feels off." My lips linger on her forehead.

Pulling back as far as my arms will allow, she gives me a brilliant smile before pressing her lips to mine. "That I can do."

I take her mouth in a scorching kiss, a silent promise to do everything in my power to protect her.

Now I just need to keep my shit together until she calls.

***

Hours later, back aching from the hours spent bent over in the chair next to Byte, I dig deep into the two men's lives. Anything to distract me from thoughts of where Kate is right now.

Worried I would wear a hole in the carpet, Byte shoved me into the extra chair in his room and told me to keep looking into the two men. Bluntly, might I add.

When the call I've been waiting for finally comes, relief sags my rigid posture as Kate chatters away in my ear. Clueless to the level of fear I suffered waiting for her call.

Or maybe she knew and this is her way of calming me down.

My lips stretch in an indulgent smile as I listen to my girl catch me up on the rest of her day.

Before letting her go, I persuade her to come to the clubhouse Saturday night.

Now to ensure she doesn't have an excuse to cancel again.

Chapter Twenty-Three

Mac

Shooting the shit at the clubhouse, all the brothers chill around the bar. I'm killing time until my girl's done catching up with Demi at the bakery. Even Byte left his cave to make a rare appearance.

The only deviation is Joker. An uncharacteristic darkness cloaks his normally affable self. Lately, his interactions with the brothers have been limited to the occasional grunt here and there.

Something's happening with him but hell if we know what. He sure as shit isn't sharing his feelings.

Bomber, taking his life in his own hands, gives a hard slap to his back just to fuck with him.

"Hey man. The ladies are bringing some new friends over tonight. You better get your ass in the shower and clean up. None of 'em are gonna go anywhere near you the way you smell right now." He taunts.

It's true. Whatever's been going on with Joker the past few weeks, showers definitely haven't been his priority.

Deciding enough is enough, I throw a dart that is sure to hit home. "Yeah, man. The ladies are too afraid to approach you right now. They figured this would be the easiest way to get you cleaned up."

My barb clearly hits its mark. "Come talk to me when you're ready to share your woman. We could have some fun between the sheets. Or hell, right out here in the open."

I'm swinging before he even finishes the taunt, my fist finding its mark, knocking Joker's ass out of his chair.

Never one to let anyone get the best of him, he's on his feet fast, taking his own swing at my face. Fist on target, my head snaps to the side with the force to my jaw.

The next thing I know he's tackled me, gaining the upper hand as the hard floor sends a spike of pain down my spine. I do my best to block his blows but he is a man possessed, pounding wherever he can reach while the brothers struggle to separate us.

"That's all you've got?" I'm playing with fire. Inciting his rage further but it's obvious my friend needs to get this aggression out.

Giving as good as him – I rear back as far as the floor allows – letting lose with another punch. A direct hit to his face.

Joker's weight disappears as Ryker drags him off me, interrupting our brawl.

"Joker! Your phone is ringing." His words break through the hostility still aimed at my prone form.

I hop to my feet as every man in the room watches Joker snatch up his phone, shamelessly listening to his one-sided conversation.

If the tensing of his body is any indication, it is not good news. Attempting to walk away without a word, he heads for the door before Ryker steps up to stop him.

"What's wrong?" Ryker asks the question we all want to know.

"Get out of my way, Prez." Joker snarls.

"Sounds like something is wrong. So, I'll let the disrespect slide this time but brother you need to tell us what's happening." Ryker continues in a calm tone.

"Sarah needs me, man. DeLuca showed up at the house and knocked her around. Said he was looking for something but she had no idea what." Assuming they're finished, Joker moves to go around him but Ryker matches him step for step to block the door. "Prez, move out of my way. I need to get over there."

"To do what, Joker? You said it yourself, she doesn't want anything to do with us." He tries to reason with him.

"Sometimes you need to force someone to accept help even when they refuse it. Man, you know this better than any of us."

Showing no reaction to Joker's harsh words, Ryker studies him for another minute before turning to the rest of us.

"Let's roll out, men. Our brother needs our help." With those few words, Ryker once again shows why he's our leader. No matter the bullshit one of the brothers throws at him, he doesn't let it sway his loyalty or piss him off.

Every brother in the clubhouse follows Ryker's order, immediately heading out to mount our bikes. We fly down the road, hoping to catch DeLuca before he disappears.

While the rest of us are looking for answers, Joker's sole focus is on the wife. And DeLuca.

I don't blame the brother at all for wanting a piece of the bastard.

Arriving at the house in record time, we move up the walkway as a well-oiled machine. Our years of military training ingrained in every move we make.

The door flies open before we reach the porch. Sarah rushes out, tears streaming down her cheeks, one of them sporting a nasty bruise.

Joker snatches her up in his arms.

From the sight of that bruise, it wasn't a loving reunion with her husband.

"Is he still here?" Interrupting their embrace, Ryker steps forward to address Sarah.

She lifts frightened eyes to Joker. "He left when I threatened to call the cops."

We all do our best to ignore her tears, giving her a moment to compose herself. Her body trembles. Most likely a dump of adrenaline after the confrontation with her douchebag husband.

Joker's hand gently cups her cheek opposite the bruise. The gentleness of his touch a stark contradiction to his usual playfulness with women. "Pack your stuff, you and the kids are coming with us."

After a short argument – all the brothers could have told her it was pointless – Joker leads her back into the house. The rest of us follow behind.

"Are your kids here?" I ask the question we all want to know, really hoping they didn't see their dad assault their mom.

If he did, he's gonna have an entire club of men after his ass. But then again, what he did to his wife isn't gonna be left unpunished.

"No, my neighbor takes them to the park with her kids a couple times a week. They should be back soon." Just then a knock sounds at the door, proving her correct.

The door swings open to a woman probably ten years older than Sarah. The two young kids must be Sarah's. The little boy sleeping in her arms looks to be around two years old. The girl, four or five at the most, tries to pull her hand from the woman to run to her mom.

"Mommy!"

"Sarah, are you okay?" The neighbor's hesitant voice – and death grip on the little girl – clearly shows her fear.

Her reaction isn't surprising. The people around here are still wary of us. Gossip spreads. Even this far from Frostown.

"Jeanette, this is my friend Joker. And his friends." Sarah lifts her arm in Joker's direction while making introductions.

He extends a hand to Jeanette, his charming smile meant to ease her fear. "Nice to meet you, ma'am."

"They're here to help me get away from Vinny." Sarah adds.

Jeanette's attitude does a one-eighty at Sarah's words. "It's about time. Do you need anything?" We all hear the relief lacing her words. She's definitely worried about her friend.

"Could you keep Joey and Lily distracted while I pack?" Sarah asks.

"Of course, anything you need. We'll be at my house whenever you're ready." She herds the kids back out the door.

Things move quickly as we help Sarah pack their stuff, none of the brothers want to chance DeLuca returning with Sarah and the kids still here.

Danger stays behind to watch the house in case the douchebag does return. The rest head out of the neighborhood in less than ten minutes, Sarah and kids in tow. We'll put them up in a room at the clubhouse for protection until this shit with her husband is resolved.

It's not the ideal solution but it's the best we can do for now.

Seeing Joker's reaction to what that bastard did to his wife – I'm relieved Kate is far away from this shit today.

I'm just grateful my girl is safe.

Chapter Twenty-Four

Kate

It's finally Friday and the weekend is calling my name. I can't escape the gates of the school fast enough.

Hello weekend!

I'm so excited to see Demi, I practically skip down Main Street. With how busy my week has been, I haven't had time for my usual drop ins at the bakery.

I miss my friend and am so looking forward to catching up with her.

I barely catch myself when my feet stumble on the sidewalk. Everything in me stuck on the friend label.

It's been years since I've had friends – more like acquaintances – and never any as close as Demi has become since I met her only a few short weeks ago.

Not that she gave me much choice in the matter. No, Demi bulldozed right through my barriers, forcing her way into my life.

She is exactly what my lonely existence needed and I didn't even know it.

The thought doesn't scare me. Instead, a wide smile stretches my face. I probably look a little loony but ask me if I care.

Not one bit.

With a new lightness, I continue my dorky skip through the door and right up to the counter.

Looks like my timing is perfect. Demi is literally finishing her closing routine when I hop to a stop.

I'm not usually excited about what day of the week it is but today is a different day.

My, how my outlook has changed.

Before meeting Mac and Demi, it didn't really make a difference. My routine was the same no matter what.

"Hey girl! What're you doing here? I figured you'd be busy with your man." Her effortless smile graces her face.

"Demi." Her name is a warning she doesn't heed. She never does.

"What? Don't even try to deny it. I've seen you together. If that's not your man, then I must be crazy."

Shaking my head at her ridiculousness, I turn the attention off myself. "Any luck finding help?"

"Ugh, no. The number of weirdos in this town is scary. I've had three guys come in just the last couple days. They spent the entire time talking to my tits. I don't think any of them actually made eye contact."

"Really?" A surprised snort of laugher escapes with my question.

That's surprising.

Not the part about staring. My friend is beautiful. Surprising that they weren't more gentlemanly. Especially if they were looking for a job.

"Don't even get me started on some of the others. Unfortunately, my search continues. I'll just have to keep working twenty-four seven until an angel appears. Or, you know, a normal person. I'll take either at this point. I need a break. Anyway, what's up? Did we have plans I forgot about?"

Her change of subject isn't surprising. She might like being in the spotlight, but that is all about her actions. When it comes to talking about herself, she is the last one to open up.

"No. I came by to see what your plans are tomorrow night." I ask her.

"A glass of wine and some me time." From the wistfulness in her expression – and all the grumbling she does about it – I know she doesn't get much of that.

"Can I tempt you into going to the clubhouse with me?" I test out my best puppy dog eyes. "Mac invited me to their party tomorrow and I'm not too sure about going alone."

"You won't be alone, that man of yours isn't going to let you leave his side once he lays eyes on you." She's exaggerating.

Mac and I aren't that serious. Right?

"Come on. You know you want to show Ryker what he's missing." I am not above begging. Hopefully, it doesn't come down to that.

"Hmm, maybe. Although, what he's not going to miss is my knee to his junk if he throws attitude my way again." From the deviousness of her smile, I am so glad I'm on her good side.

I bet she gets downright diabolical when provoked.
She gives me a long considering look. "Okay, I'm in. Meet at your house?" I didn't realize how nervous I was until she finally relents.
"Perfect. Seven? I have a new client to visit in the afternoon, but I should be done by then." I say.
Details ironed out, we chat for a few more minutes before I need to head home. I want to check in with April. Our relationship has been strained since our argument last week and I have no clue what to do about it.

Chapter Twenty-Five

Kate

The next night I am once again on a mission, frantically searching my closet for something to wear.

What the heck do I have that would be appropriate for a party at a motorcycle clubhouse?

Nothing, that's what.

I really need to go shopping.

Demi's offer to dress me was promptly declined. Adamantly.

Her expression was filled with a little too much deviousness when she made the offer.

I'm learning my lesson with that girl.

Give her an inch and she'll take the whole darn mile.

Flinging hangers aside, I know there has got to be something in my closet that is not too conservative. I definitely do not want to go all out but there must be some middle ground in here.

Maybe I should have let Demi have her way with my wardrobe.

Just when I am ready to give up, a flash of green in the very back catches my eye.

"Score!" The green halter top from the one party my college roommate dragged me to is perfect. I'm pretty sure this night will turn out much better than the last time I wore it.

With time running out, no doubt Demi will be right on time, I throw it on the bed, deciding to pair it with some skinny jeans and flats. Heels are way out of my wheelhouse.

I can definitely work with that.

Demi's knock at the door sounds right as I am hopping into my jeans, desperately ignoring the fact it takes a little more effort these days.

Might need to lay off the sinful goodies for a while.

"Coming!" I yell to be heard from the bedroom, hurrying to pull my boots on while rushing to open the door.

Demi struts through the open front door in a dress.

If you can call that scrap of material attempting to cover her body a dress.

No shame in her game.

"Wow. You look amazing." And she really does. She has a confidence I envy. I have no idea how she isn't self-conscious in so little.

The strapless dress shows off her tattoos. Running shoulders to wrists, full-sleeves on both arms. The tasteful artwork is a swirl of beautifully vibrant colors and I am sure tell a story she isn't ready to share yet.

I suspect each one was inked with significant meaning but Demi is tightlipped about her past, so I don't know for sure.

She is a knockout and she knows it.

"Thanks, girl! You don't look so bad yourself." She runs her eyes over me in approval. "You looking to start a brawl? Mac won't be the only one unable to tear his eyes off you."

Cue the heat in my cheeks. Her blunt honesty gets my blush going as usual.

Deciding I don't have the brain power to feed into her outrageousness, I ask a question of my own to distract her. "Ready to go?"

"Yes!" Her excitement is infectious. I give her my first genuine smile of the night as we exit the house. My nerves have been completely out of control all day.

April is still distant and I have no idea what to do about it. This is a first for us. We have *always* been able to talk through whatever issues we face. I am at a loss. Maybe I pushed too hard.

Add that to my first trip to a motorcycle club party and my nerves are shot. From the books I read, I know a little of what to expect. Hopefully, it won't be too bad.

The ride to the clubhouse flies by as Demi regales me with hilarious stories about setting up the bakery. Crazy issues she never expected to encounter that had her doubting her ability to succeed.

I am so grateful she persevered. That she didn't disappear from Frostown before I had the chance to walk into her bakery. I never would have met her if her sweet treats didn't entice me into her shop that fateful day.

Nerves mostly gone by the time we arrive, I acknowledge her scheme to calm me down with an appreciative smile.

With a deep breath, I push through the doors of the clubhouse.

The scene unfolding in front of me makes me wish I never left the house.

Oh my.

Chapter Twenty-Six

Kate

It's like their very own live porn show.

My brain can't decide where to look. What to focus on.

All around us, couples are in different states of sexual activity. Men and women paired off, different variations of threesomes – all in various levels of undress.

Try as I might, I cannot tear my eyes off the wicked exhibitions in front of us.

How did I let Mac convince me this was a good idea?

My wide-eyed stare snags on Mac across the room. The casual way he leans on the bar, talking with his brothers, it's obvious this is not a rare occurrence around here.

His hawk-like gaze is zeroed in on me like he clocked me as soon as I walked through the door. Like he knows I am ready to bolt.

His electric blue eyes, impossible to ignore, ignite a fire in my core as they roam my body like a lover's caress. I feel it from clear across the room.

Memories of how he plays my body like a maestro roll through my head.

Is it hot in here? Feels like the temperature just rose a hundred degrees.

Crooking his finger, it's clear he expects me to traverse the sexual escapades to get to him.

Don't be a coward, Kate.

Taking a deep inhale for courage, I grab Demi's hand to drag her through the sensual scene with me. Also, to ensure my adventurous friend doesn't abandon me to join the sexual escapades.

I love my friend but that is not *a visual I ever want in my head.*

What feels like an eternity later, Demi's voice rises over the music when we reach the bar. "Damn boys. You sure know how to party. I thought I knew what to expect but my experience has nothing on this!"

Mine aren't the only surprised eyes that fly to my friend at her unexpected revelation.

No, she garners the attention of all the men standing around the bar.

Demi's been around an MC before?

My friend just gets more interesting the longer I'm around her.

"Damn girl! Where have you been all my life and will you marry me?" Joker teases.

If the scowl on Ryker's face is any indication, he does not seem as happy to see her. "What are you doing here?"

With a flick of her wrist, she waves away his displeasure, giving him a smoldering smile. "Um, my friend invited me. She thought I could show you boys how to have a good time."

I am so engrossed in their drama, it takes a minute to notice the slide of Mac's arm around my waist. Once I do, it's impossible to ignore the sparks lighting me up when his hard body brushes my backside.

Standing to his full height, he uses that arm to turn me away from the show. He retakes his seat, tugging me even close to nestle between his hard thighs.

I can't say I'll ever complain about his preferred perch for me. All those hard muscles wrapped around me. The move makes me feel protected. Cherished.

Definitely not feelings I've had much experience with.

I watch with wide eyes as even more people pour through the doors. Mac's hand on my cheek draws my attention back to him, waiting for me to make eye contact before he leans down to press a soft lingering kiss on my lips.

I'm sure he can feel the nerves rolling off me in waves.

"Siren, I missed you." The diversion helps as I get lost in his heated eyes. The activities in the room momentarily forgotten.

That is, until the loud bickering next to us breaks me out of my Mac daze.

I tune back in to hear Ryker interrogating Demi, demanding to know what other MC she spent time with.

"Baby, that's for me to know." Of course, she just can't help herself, carrying on flirtatiously. "And you to find out only if you're lucky."

Even I can see my friend is playing with fire. Ryker looks like he's about to blow a gasket.

I think I actually see smoke rising.

If she's not careful, the fuming biker is going to go all caveman and drag her out of here.

Probably by her hair.

"Demi."

Demi, of course, ignores his warning growl. Actually, she completely ignores him and turns to the bar instead. "We need shots!"

I'm not too sure about doing shots with Demi. Not after our night at Dean's. And not with all the porn going on around us.

"I don't think so. No shots for me tonight. I'll stick with wine." I shut her down before she tries to push the shot glass in my hand.

"Girl, you're no fun. Who else is gonna do shots with me?" She pouts.

"Find Jade or the other girls." I tell her.

Her pout isn't working on me tonight.

She turns her back to the bar with a frown – most likely looking for the girls.

She's still pointedly ignoring Ryker, who hasn't taken his glare off her for a second. "Woman, you know I'm standing right here."

"Yeah, I know. You're blocking my search for a dance partner." My friend is fearless in the face of the deadly man that would send me running right back out the door if he was aiming that look at me.

I think that's steam coming out his ears.

"Careful Prez. Don't want you blowing a gasket." Joker taunts.

Mac squeezes my hips, pulling my attention back to him. I have no idea what is going on with those two and I'm not sure I want to.

"You want red or white wine?" He asks.

"Red is good."

He calls out my order to the prospect behind the bar.

With the crowd tonight, it takes a few minutes before my drink is placed on the bar in front of me.

A fortifying sip cools my overheated body.

"Whoa. Slow down, Siren. We have all night." Mac cautions.

Okay so it wasn't a sip. I gulped half that sucker down.

Sue me.

Fighting the urge to down the rest, I set the glass on the bar.

"Relax babe." He says when he wraps his arm around me again, after moving the temptation further out of my reach.

Jade appears at Mac's side before I can defend myself.

"Kate, I'm so glad you came!" Her enthusiasm spreads warmth in my tummy. *That might be the wine.*

Still, I'm happy to see her. I lean as far as Mac will let me to return her hug. "Hi Jade. It's so good to see you again."

"I was just telling the girls we need to go shopping. You should come with." Eyes bright, I'm not sure if it's the alcohol talking or if she truly wants to hang out with me.

"You want me to go with you?" I ask.

"Yes! We'll do a girls day. It'll be fun!" She must be drunk. I have no idea why else she would be so excited to spend time with my boring self.

Before I even finish the thought, my inner voice chastises.

There is something seriously wrong with you. These girls think there is something special about you. Hasn't your shyness held you back long enough?

For once, my inner voice isn't too outrageous, so I take a leap. "You know, you're right. That's a great idea. I was just telling myself I need some new clothes."

Mac's voice joins the conversation. "Siren, there's nothing wrong with your clothes. I like this top. It matches your eyes."

Cue the warm fuzzies.

"It is beautiful and shows off that amazing body." Jade's opinion swiftly turns Mac's indulgent smile to a scowl. I think he just realized he isn't the only man getting a view of my body.

Hmm, maybe Demi was spot on. Hope a brawl doesn't break out.

Attempting to defuse his irritation, I steer the conversation back to plans of shopping. "Let me know when you're planning to go. As long as I'm not working at the school, I should be able to work around my clients."

"Sounds good. I'll text you when we decide." She disappears into the crowd as quickly as she appeared.

"Speaking of clients, how's it goin' with Mrs. Smith?" Mac asks.

"She's such a sweetheart." I spend the next few minutes animatedly telling him about my first visit with her. "I don't think I'll learn anything about Michael from her but she definitely needs my help."

He doesn't look too happy about how well we got on. "Mac, she's harmless. Nothing is going to happen to me when I'm with her."

"Baby, I don't want anything happening to you, period." He pulls me closer like he's afraid something is going to happen right this second.

"You doing okay with the party? We can leave if it's too much." His question shows he cares about more than just my physical well-being.

"I'm good." He's sweet to check. "I'm glad you warned me before I came." Bolstered by liquid courage, I mistakenly glance behind me to survey the room again.

Jade has been a busy girl.

Sandwiched between Bomber and Rocker, she might as well be topless in the middle of the dance floor. Her body sways seductively between the two men.

Her backside gyrates suggestively against Bomber's crotch while Rocker plays with her nipples barely visible where he's pulled her top down. Bomber's face, buried in her neck, partially blocks my view of the erotic kiss she's locked in with Rocker.

"Oh my God!" My exclamation snags Mac's attention. He pivots on his stool to see what has me riveted.

"Do you want to leave?" He whispers the question across the shell of my ear.

"Not yet." I answer with a shiver, goosebumps breaking out across my entire body.

So fixated on the erotic show, I don't notice his arms slipping around my sides until he cups my breasts in his large hands.

I reach my hands up automatically, intending to stop him.

My entire body freezes, watching motionless as Rocker breaks the kiss to lick his way down Jade's breast before sucking a hard nipple into his mouth.

Even from a distance, the suction looks strong as most of her breast disappears into his mouth. Her hand sinks into the hair at the back of his neck. It's a mystery whether she's pulling him close or pushing him away.

She looks like she's in pain.

"Are you imagining that it's you?" Mac asks. "Caught up between two hard bodies." Any protest dies when he pinches my hard nipples. A wave of arousal so strong I almost come on the spot arrows straight to my clit. "Don't lie to me." Sensing my surrender, he continues his verbal torture. "Your hard little nipples tell me the truth. Do you want my mouth on you, Siren?"

A sliver of sanity remains, stopping me from letting Mac turn the fantasy into reality for everyone to see.

I somehow tear my gaze away from the eroticism playing out on the dance floor, forcing myself to turn and face him.

"Your room?" It takes all the brain cells I have right now to force those two words out of my mouth.

With one last pinch to my nipples, Mac releases my breasts and stands.

Thankfully, his guiding hand leads me through the room. Anticipation is a living, breathing beast consuming me.

I'm powerless to keep my eyes from straying to the erotic trio, riveted to the sight of Bomber unbuttoning Jade's jeans before his hand disappears inside.

I am a captivated voyeur as we enter the hallway. Her moans echo behind us as I lose sight of the show.

Chapter Twenty-Seven

Kate

Mac slams the door to his room, the lock sounding like a shot in the darkness. He picks me up and shoves me against the hard wood, my body instinctively wrapping around him. Legs around his waist. Arms anchored around his neck. I hold on for the ride, my inhibitions lost to the arousal burning me from the inside out.

"Siren, you're soaked. Your little pussy is on fire, isn't it?" He doesn't give me time to respond.

No, he presses his hardness right into my core. Right where I need him most.

"Tell me what you want, baby."

Still lost in a sexual haze, there's only one word I can force past my numb lips. "You."

"Where do you want me? Give me the words." The roll of his hips serves only to build my desire higher, tingles of awareness overwhelming me.

"I-" In my haze, I struggle to put my jumbled thoughts into coherent words.

"You want my dick?" The nod I give isn't enough for him. This glorious man wants to incinerate me. "Where do you want my dick?"

I finally find my voice. "Inside me."

"Mmmm. Me too, Siren."

His mouth plays at my neck, sharp nips and suckling licks on my sensitive skin. All serving to fry my brain. Send electric pulses straight to my core.

But he's not done testing my limits. "Where inside you?" He pushes me to voice my desires.

The alluring play of his mouth on my neck makes coherent thought impossible. Unbidden, my hips swivel, a dirty rotation of pleasure rubbing my core directly over his jean-covered hardness.

"You want my dick in your pussy?" He's relentless, gripping the hair at the base of my neck. Pulling hard to bring my face around to meet the intensity in his blue eyes.

"Yes!" My cry echoes in the room, unable to tear my gaze from the smoldering blue flames.

"Tell me. I want to hear the words." Doesn't he know his dirty words, his naughty mouth attacking my neck, are *so* not helping me form coherent thoughts. Or words for that matter.

Needing him like I need air to breathe gives me the courage to force the words out.

With a deep breath – and a lot of mental effort – I maintain eye contact, push the words past my lips. "I want. Oh God. I want you in my pussy."

"What do you want in your pussy?" The man is a torturous tease.

Hesitating, I finally give him what he wants. "Your dick."

"Where do you want my dick?"

"I want your dick in my pussy." This time it's easier to let the full sentence fall from my lips.

My desire hangs in the air between us.

"Good girl." Mac releases his hold on my butt allowing my legs to descend to the floor. His hands gently grasp my arms until I'm steady on my feet.

I wait in breathless suspense for his next move.

"Turn around, Siren." He commands.

Following his direction, his hard body envelops me completely. The rasp of his scruff an intimate stroke over my cheek that arrows directly to my clit. Pleasure pulses. Desire mounts.

Adding to my sensory overload, his calloused hands coast around my waist, over the sliver of skin exposed where my halter doesn't meet my jeans. The sizzling feel of his rough skin on my softer body a dichotomous contradiction.

Mac teases the tips of his fingers along the edge of my jeans before slipping inside to tease the sensitive skin at the edge of my panties.

Whimpers escape. Uncontrollable. I'm reduced to a babbling mess as he plays my body.

What feels like an eternity later, he grasps the button of my jeans. The loosening of the material at my hips precedes the sound of my zipper ever so slowly sliding down.

"Bend over and slide them off. Panties too." My hands move without direction from my brain.

Wetness weeps from my core at his harsh command, escaping to soak my panties. And heat to warm my cheeks. Thankfully, he can't see either. Not yet at least.

I glide my thumbs into the sides of my jeans and panties before taking a deep breath. Then I slowly slide them over my hips. The contrast of the rough material on my sensitive skin is just another layer of sensation building my desire to a fever pitch.

Following his instructions, I keep my legs straight and bend at the waist to drop both to the floor.

All the while fighting the embarrassment of the picture I must make in this moment.

"Stop. Stay just like that." He orders. "You're beautiful."

Oh God.

He steps closer, taking hold of my hips, hands slowly mapping my shape. His journey ends with a firm squeeze of my cheeks.

Grateful I'm facing away from him, my cheeks are on fire now.

Probably the ones in his hands too.

And he's not done. He spreads me open. Reveals the height of my arousal as the cool air of the room blows over the cream covering my inner thighs. Fingers gliding through the lips of my sex, Mac spreads it around my sensitive flesh. His booted foot enters my view, stepping on the discarded material between my legs as he guides me to step out of them.

I don't have long to wait for his next order. "Back up."

I'm helpless with my back to him. The anticipation of his next move or order is an erotic assault ambushing my senses.

I jolt at the sudden pull on my hips. A mortifying yelp escapes as we fall back on the bed. Somehow, he maneuvers my legs to straddle his body.

Before I realize his intent, he's forcing my hips higher until my sex settles over his face.

What the heck? How in the world did he pull that off?

It's like a choreographed porn move.

I lose all train of thought when he sucks my clit into his mouth. The harsh pull quickly blanks my mind.

Embarrassment flees as I lose myself in the euphoric experience. Gyrating and grinding above him, I chase his mouth for the pressure I need most.

His moves are leisurely. Like we have all the time in the world.

Like he's savoring his favorite meal.

Slow and measured, he has no idea how close to the precipice I already am. My body greedily seeks the pleasure I can only find with Mac.

My orgasm is an eruption of radiant light that catches me completely by surprise. Waves of pleasure cascade through my entire body.

"So sweet. So responsive."

He releases the suction on my clit. Softening the pressure to slow licks of his tongue up and down the lips of my sex.

He doesn't give me long to recover. I watch through lust glazed eyes as he quickly reaches down to push his jeans past his hips all while pulling a condom from his pocket.

I am entranced as he situates the condom even as the soft glide of his tongue continues to tease me. Already, my desire builds again. The erotic sight of his fist gripping his hardness. Pumping once. Twice. Much harder than I've ever thought to give.

Once sheathed, he shifts me down his body until my sex hovers over his hardness.

With one hard thrust, he seats himself fully inside me. It's a stark contrast to the gentleness of his hands on my hips.

"Ride me, Siren." His strong hands squeeze my hips. The black ink on his hands dancing as he guides my movements.

With small tentative circles, I gain confidence when his rumbled groan sounds behind me. "That's it. Use me, baby. Take your pleasure."

My rotating hips pick up speed as a second orgasm builds unexpectedly.

Lost in the chase of my own pinnacle of pleasure.

Except for Mac, I have never had more than one orgasm during sex. And never during penetration.

The sex God below me proves me wrong. He knows exactly where to hit that spot inside to send me soaring into the stratosphere.

"Come for me, Siren. I want to feel your pussy strangling my dick."

My orgasm explodes at his command. Tingles radiate out from my core. Stars flash in my vision.

The rhythmic squeeze of my muscles pulls Mac over the edge with me.

I'm a boneless heap on top of him, but he doesn't seem to mind as he turns us to nestle me into the curve of his arm. The pounding of his heart soothes me with a hypnotic beat.

I feel cherished for the first time in my life.

All thanks to the breathtaking man wrapping me in his arms like he'll never let go.

Chapter Twenty-Eight

Mac

As I lay here catching my breath, recovering from the best sex of my life, the perfection of Kate's boneless weight plastered to my chest sears this moment in my memory forever. Her soft body the perfect fit to my hardness.

That is, until her tentative voice breaks through my euphoric daydream. "Mac."

"Hmm?" I mumble.

"I don't want to have sex in front of other people." The uncertainty in her voice brings me crashing back down to Earth.

Well, fuck. That definitely isn't what I wanted either.

Weaving my fingers in her hair, I grasp the strands to lift her head from where she has buried her face. I patiently wait for her eyes to connect with mine. My voice remains silent as I watch her gather her courage to look at me.

"Siren, we don't do anything you're not comfortable with." I reassure her. "I know watching Bomber and Rocker tease Jade got you hot. Just because the fantasy turns you on, does not mean the real thing will do it for you. It is just that, a fantasy.

"There is absolutely nothing wrong with getting turned on by the thought of multiple partners laser focused on your pleasure. But if it is not something you want, it won't happen." I let the truth shine through my eyes. A silent promise that there is nothing wrong with indulging in what turns you on.

My pleasure is driven by her pleasure. Seeing her get off, gets me off. Plain and simple.

"I won't deny I have been with a lot of women. I'm no saint. Dirty talk gets me hot and even with the blushes your body can't hide, I think you like it too."

Snuggling back down into my chest, she hides her face in my pecs again. Hiding herself from me. Afraid to admit that it turns her on.

That is just unacceptable.

"Baby, you don't need to be embarrassed. Everyone has fantasies." I try to reassure her. "Anyone that tells you they don't is a damn liar. What we do is nothing to be ashamed of."

She nods her head and I console myself that it's the best I am going to get tonight.

Baby steps.

Patience is key with my Siren. I'll show her every day until she believes me. Believes in us. Believes in herself.

When her mouth opens against my skin – I know before she speaks – she's ready to change the subject. "Why do you call me Siren?" She asks.

"Because as much bad as I have done in my life, you still have the power to tempt me into more. Even though I know it could lead to my ruin, I just don't have a choice when it comes to you." I admit, giving her more truth than she may be ready for but I just can't hold it back.

I reach over to turn off the light. Pulling her more comfortably into the crook of my arm, I return to my peaceful doze from moments ago. "Let's get some sleep." I've dropped a lot on her tonight.

Give her time. She'll come around.

Foreign sensations urge me to wrap myself around her and never let go. I'll protect this woman with my life. To my very last day if she'll let me. It's a feeling I have never felt with another woman before. With Kate, it just feels as natural as breathing.

Feeling a lot like protectiveness – and dare I say love – the emotions don't scare me like I always assumed they would.

What does scare me? The thought of losing her. That scares the shit out of me and I will do everything in my power to keep that from happening.

Jade was right, she is the perfect softness to smooth my hard edges.

The effortless way we fit together settles a peace I have never known right down to my soul as we drift off to sleep. Patience will be my best friend as I wait for her to trust me.

And she will. I'll make sure of it.

One word circles on repeat in my brain.

Mine. Mine. Mine.

And I never want to let her go.

I will do everything in my power to keep her.

No matter the cost.

Chapter Twenty-Nine

Kate

Sunlight streams through the window, stirring me from the best sleep I've had in ages.

Maybe even ever.

My poor muscles, in desperate need of a stretch, move languorously across the soft sheets of Mac's bed. A contented sigh escapes when my backside connects with the hard muscled body behind me.

A month ago, I would have stiffened against him but now my body unconsciously seeks his warmth in the chilly autumn mornings. These last weeks have been a whirlwind of stolen moments when I can break away from my responsibilities.

Even though our schedules don't align often, we've made the most of our time together, seeing each other a few nights a week doing couple-y things.

He's a bit of a food connoisseur. More specifically – lover of off the beaten path homestyle cooking. His mission is to expand my horizons with hole-in-the-wall burger joints and crumbling buildings hiding the best BBQ I've ever had.

And that was only last week.

In return, I've given him a personal tour of little known treasures around the town I grew up in.

And the sex. OMG. The sex is off the charts.

He is a sorcerer enticing me into some compromising exploits at every turn. Just the thought of the carnal wantonness he coaxes out of me. My core constricts, cream escaping to soak my panties, heat flooding my cheeks.

He is temptation personified that I have no hope of resisting.

I love the time we spend together just doing normal things but my absolute favorite is the long rides on his motorcycle.

There is a peace in trusting his control as we ride through the neighboring mountains. The exhilaration of the wind whipping by, my body pressed tight to him. All my worries fade away.

There is no better feeling in the world.

Who would have thought the girl who had never been on a motorcycle would turn out to love it almost as much as her man?

The only dark cloud is my time volunteering. Mac asked me to take a step back to give us more time together but I just can't stomach the thought of leaving my clients hanging.

We're currently at an impasse.

Mac's arm tightens like a band around my waist as he stirs, burying his face in my hair, his deep inhale ruffling my hairline as he trails soft kisses. "Good morning, Siren."

"Mmm, good morning." I whisper.

His gravelly morning voice never fails to send shivers of awareness rippling down my spine. "Sleep good?"

"Yes. Never better." My voice is a soft murmur as I struggle to fully wake up, my body completely boneless thanks to the man holding me.

"Good." He makes no effort to hide the unmistakable masculine pride in his voice.

Mac slides the tips of his fingers slowly down the soft skin of my arm, goosebumps left in his wake.

It's an intimate moment.

More so than the times we've had sex. Almost like an assurance he's with me.

I won't lie. It scares me.

This overwhelming need to lean on someone else.

"I need to get up. I have a lot to do today." For once, I wish I didn't have so much on my plate. If, just for today, I could spend the day lazing in bed exploring the perfection of Mac's body.

"Are you sure you can't stay? I can make it worth your while." I shiver at the whispered words softly brushing over my sensitive skin.

"I wish I could." The words are a struggle to push past my lips.

Who knew my voice could purr like that? Certainly not me.

Rough fingertips map a path of heat over the fleshy curve of my hip.

He is so *not* helping my struggle.

"Okay. I guess I'll let you go. Will you have breakfast with me first?" He asks.

"That I can do." I agree.

Another teasing nibble, the abrasion of his rough beard on my shoulder, has me second guessing my decision.

Before I can change my mind, Mac pushes himself up, taking his comforting heat away.

With a pout, I roll to my back, letting the sheet fall to my waist. The view of my bare breasts a homing beacon that stops him in his tracks as his eyes lock on the sight with hunger.

"Careful, Siren. I already don't want to let you out of this bed. You keep flashing that gorgeous body at me, I'll say fuck it and devour you the rest of the day." He grates out, voice full of dark promise.

My body heats at the brazenness of his words. His predatory gaze. The red hue of my blush is impossible to hide in my exposed position. Starting from the tips of my breasts and spreading up to end at my cheeks.

I have no hope of hiding it with the fairness of my skin. His patented smirk tells me exactly how much he enjoys the effect he has on me.

I honestly believe he does it on purpose.

Taking no chances, I roll to the opposite side of the bed. The silence of my phone mocks me when I pick it up from the nightstand.

April has been keeping her distance still. Thoughts of her burst the happy bubble that is my time with Mac.

I wish once again for more time in the day so I can be there for everyone that needs me. I am spread so thin right now and I don't know how to change that.

My anxiety crashes back in full force. My fear of failing is a noose tightening my insides. "Mac, I really should get going."

"Come on, babe. You need to eat." His words are muffled by the shirt he pulls over his head.

"Okay but something quick. I really do need to go." I acquiesce.

He's right. I do need to eat if I want to power through my day.

Childish giggles reverberate down the hall as soon as Mac opens his door. I'm sure surprise is written all over my face as my eyes fly to his. It never crossed my mind there might be children in the clubhouse.

"It's a long story." Mac's hand falls to my lower back, guiding me down the hallway. "Let's go introduce you to our guests."

A whirlwind of activity greets us in the main room of the clubhouse. A petite blond stands at the kitchen doorway with an indulgent smile as she watches an adorable little boy ride the back of a biker while an equally adorable girl gives chase.

Is that Joker?

"Umm." I'm not really sure what I'm seeing here.

Mac laughs in the face of my confusion. "Don't ask."

We carefully cross the room to avoid interfering with the kids' endearing playtime.

"Kate, this is Sarah. Those are her kids making an ass of Joker." Mac introduces me to the blond when we reach her side.

"Hi Sarah. It's nice to meet you." I hold my hand out to her with a genuine smile.

Taking my hand in a shaky grip, her smile morphs to a more reserved one. Much different than the secretive one she watched the trio behind us with. "Hi, Kate. Nice to meet you too."

The awkward introduction is broken by a weird sound and childish giggles.

Is that neighing?

"They're adorable." My own burst of laughter joins in as I glance at the man-child behind us doing his best horse interpretation.

She lights up at the compliment, some of the apprehension leaves her expression. A radiant glow takes its place, lighting her from within.

A second later, the little girl almost knocks her off her feet when she barrels into her legs.

"Mommy! Did you see Joker give me a horsey ride?" Resting her chin on Sarah's thigh, she gazes adoringly up at her.

"I did baby girl. It looked like you had a fun ride." The love between them is tangible as Sarah stares down at who I assume is her daughter. "Lily. This is Kate."

The adorable face staring up at me steals my heart. I drop down to kneel at her level and hold my hand out to her. "Hi, Lily. It's nice to meet you."

Much more enthusiastically than her mother, Lily slides her tiny hand into mine with a toothy grin. "You're so pretty."

My cheeks warm at her awed compliment.

Seems my embarrassment isn't immune to innocent children's compliments either.

Thankfully, we're interrupted when Joker jogs over with the little boy on his shoulders. "Hey, Kate. Have you met Joey?"

Rolling my lips between my teeth, it takes a minute to compose myself in the face of Joker's ridiculousness.

I get my hilarity under control just enough to answer him. "No, I haven't. I was just introducing myself to Lily."

Straightening to my full height, I still have a long way to look up at the adorable little boy on his shoulders. "Hi, Joey. It's nice to meet you."

He buries his cute little face on the opposite side of Joker's head, effectively hiding himself from us.

"We got a shy one here." Joker says. "Joey doesn't know what to do in the presence of a beautiful woman." It's said with a wink in our direction.

Most likely to avoid the clenched fist Mac looks to be ready to throw at him.

"So, how about you help me convince Sarah how awesome it will be to take the kids to the pumpkin patch this weekend?"

"Sorry, not sure how much help I'll be. My family never went to one." Yet another thing my father considered trivial.

"Siren, that's all the more reason to go. We'll get April to go with us. You two could use some good old fashioned fun." Mac suggests.

"I don't know, Mac. I still have a lot to do tomorrow. I don't really have the time to take away from my work." It's not something I have ever considered doing as an adult.

"Baby, you need to make time for some fun. It's Sarah and the kids' first time too. It'll be good for you and April to do something together." Mac presses.

Guilt weighs on my conscious at that. Adding Mac to my already busy schedule has made it that much harder to find time to spend with April.

We're both so busy, it's not often April and I are free to spend time together. Neither of us have even had the time to catch up on our reality TV backlog.

"Let me talk to her and see if she's free. What time are you planning on going?" Maybe it will be the perfect olive branch to get past the awkward tension between us.

"The kids usually nap between noon and two. So, any time after that works for us." Interestingly, it's Joker that answers. "Sarah doesn't want to go with just the men so it would be awesome if you two join us."

"Okay. I'll text you later and let you know for sure." Realizing how late I really am running now, I reach up to press a kiss to Mac's cheek. "I really do need to go now."

"Wait. Joker and the kids actually left some food from breakfast. I'll wrap something for you to take with you." Sarah is sweet to offer. "Give me just a minute."

Mac's arm anchors me to his side, effectively thwarting any attempted escape I could make while Sarah rushes back from the kitchen.

After a quick thanks for the food and a longer kiss to Mac, I hustle out of the clubhouse to tackle my to do list.

Chapter Thirty

Mac

Patience is not my friend as I pace at the entrance to the Mountain View Farm. The farm hosts the town's annual pumpkin patch about fifteen minutes outside the city limits. Kate and April should be here any time.

It's a relief that Kate convinced April to come. The strain on their relationship has been weighing on my girl lately.

April is like her little sister and I know she only wants what is best for her. This should be a great way to break the ice after their argument. With some fun thrown in.

Most of the brothers are currently paying witness to my over the top anticipation of Kate's arrival. And by most, I mean *all* since just about everyone decided to come out today.

All except Rocker. I honestly think he's afraid he'll intimidate the children here. I guess I can see that. How many children have been around six and a half feet of bald, tattooed badasses in their short lives?

Never mind that he's a big teddy bear with Sarah's little tikes. He's as bad as Joker letting them use him as their own personal playground.

The kids are disappointed their second favorite brother isn't with us. We're all doing our best to distract them from their missing friend.

I glance to the dirt parking lot in time to see Kate's car pull in. My feet carry me her direction before I even realize I'm moving. My boots kick up almost as much dust as her car with the speed I move across the dirt. I step to her car door as soon as she turns off the ignition.

Hand closing over the handle, I swing the door open and reach in to pull her out of the car. Not stopping until her soft curves are pressed against me exactly where she belongs.

She's got her hair piled on top of her head again today. The exposed column of her neck a temptation I can't resist. I bury my face in the sensitive spot, taking a deep inhale of her sweet citrusy scent. "I missed you, Siren."

"I missed you too." She's pulling herself away even as she says it. A pink blush stains her cheeks. My girl is still adjusting to public displays of affection.

I look over to April huddled at the back of the car, uncertainty stamped all over her face. Slinging my arm over Kate's shoulder, I amble toward her and extend my hand out. "Hi April. We haven't officially met. I'm Mac."

It takes a second before she responds softly. "Hi Mac. It's nice to meet you."

Her eyes flash briefly to mine before flickering away. Looks like her shyness is overwhelming her. I also sense a little lingering tension between the cousins.

"Nice to meet you too. I'm glad you and Kate were able to come today." Wanting to put her at ease, I switch the focus to the kids. "Lily and Joey are about ready to explode if we don't get in there and explore. You ladies ready?"

With nods from them both, we head over to the rest of our group. The kids barely allow any time for introductions before our odd group converges on the entrance.

Lily and Joey lead the way, Sarah and Joker just along for the ride.

As we enter the gates of the ranch, amazement stamped on the kids' faces as they take in all the different booths. The festive event offers a wide range of activities.

There is a face painting setup. Food vendors. And of course, no small-town seasonal event would be complete without a drink stand, complete with a large sign boasting a variety of unique beverage offerings to warm you up.

Not surprisingly, the kids are captivated by the large display of face painting options. The search for the perfect pumpkin momentarily forgotten as they stare up at their mom with matching looks of longing. They're just begging to start the festivities off there.

"Please Mommy!" Little voices beg in unison.

"Of course. I bet we can get your mom to get her face painted too." Joker, the sucker, has no hope of denying them anything. He wraps his arm around Sarah's shoulders to guide them over to the booth.

The first sign of April loosening up comes as she watches their little faces light up in their excitement, following behind with a small smile.

Looks like I made the right decision to invite her too.

Knowing they were raised in a super strict household, I want to ensure they have a fun day today. "Come on, Siren. Looks like your cousin is ready for a day of fun."

A few minutes later, we leave the others near the front gates, the three of us heading for the corn maze first.

I don't even care how many times we get lost as we navigate the maze.

My face hurts from my constant smile as April and Kate giggle through the endless twists and turns, running into dead end after dead end.

It doesn't matter that it takes us more than an hour to find our way out. The sheer joy on their faces is completely worth it.

Kate gazes up at me like a kid in a candy store when we finally find our way out. "That was awesome!"

While still somewhat reserved, over the course of the day, April has slowly begun to emerge from her shell. Almost all traces of shyness have faded.

While Kate is distracted helping Sarah and the kids find the perfect pumpkins, I seize the opportunity to sidle up to April.

"I'm glad you came today. It's good to see you and Kate spending time together. Having fun." I tell her.

"I'm glad I came too. She works so much. It's good to see her taking a break." There's still a little wariness on her face but she seems receptive.

In that, we're in complete agreement. "Yeah. I've been trying to get her to back down on some of her volunteer hours but she won't hear of it."

"No. She won't. It's her true passion. I wish I could take some of the burden, so she doesn't have to work so hard." April's sincerity rings true. She loves her cousin as much as Kate loves her.

"It's not just her I'm worried about. I'm here for you too. If there's anything you need, Kate's not the only one you can call." I pull out my phone and hand it to her. "If you don't mind, I'd like to exchange numbers in case there's anything you need."

She takes my phone and enters her number. I make sure to call the number when she hands it back, so she has mine too.

"I mean it, April. Anything you need." It's going to take more than words to completely overcome her wariness.

I know that.

But I'm willing to put in the effort to show her I want to add to their small family.

Not break it apart.

That goal accomplished, I stroll back over to where Kate watches Sarah and the kids with an indulgent smile. My arms automatically slip around her waist to pull her close. "You having fun, Siren?"

The radiant smile she shoots up at me answers my question before the words leave her lips.

"Yes! I didn't think I would have so much fun." Pushing up on the tips of her toes, she presses a chaste kiss to my lips. "Thank you for inviting us today. I think April had fun too."

She's beautiful in the fading sunlight, brightening my world with her radiance. She holds me captivated as she loses her worries in the festivities.

"See, it's okay to take some time away to enjoy life." I tell her, my voice gravelly.

"You're right." She shivers against me before turning back to watch the kids again.

"You cold?" Pulling her closer, I wrap her in the heat of my body. Rest my chin on top of her head.

My dick hardens uncontrollably where it's pressed to her ass. Another shiver rushes through her body.

"No. I'm not cold." Desire washes over me at her softly whispered words. The husky timbre of her voice the same as when I'm buried deep in her pussy.

I need to rein this in before it gets out of control. This is definitely not the place to be walking around with a hard dick while children run around in their innocent fun.

Regretfully giving her one last squeeze, I step away and grab her hand to head over to the refreshment booth. The rest of the afternoon is spent shooting the shit with my brothers while the women ensure the kids have the time of their lives.

Chapter Thirty-One

Mac

I'm worried. Seriously worried.

Kate has been radio silent today. I thought we were making progress after the pumpkin patch. Kate and April surprised by how much fun we had. Neither of them expected to enjoy themselves so much.

Now I wonder if my pursuit of her is coming on too strong.

My draw to her undeniable. Like nothing I've ever felt before.

Sometimes it seems like she's right there with me. Other times I have my doubts.

When multiple texts and phone calls go unanswered, I give in to the uncontrollable urge to take a ride into town to set eyes on her.

Her car is in the driveway when I roll up to the curb.

So, she is home.

Now her silence is even more concerning. A fear like nothing I have ever felt before propels me forward, just the thought of something happening to her freezing my blood.

That concern sounds loud and clear in the bang of my fist on her door. It takes a minute until, finally, I hear hobbling footsteps seconds before the door opens.

My girl leans against the doorframe with her foot wrapped in an ice pack.

"Siren. What happened?" Distress laces my voice. I push across the threshold, wrapping an arm around her waist to take some of her weight.

A grimace she has no hope of hiding crosses her face even as she attempts to paste a smile on her lips.

"It's nothing. The smoke alarm was beeping a warning. When I was changing the batteries, I stepped off the ladder wrong. I think it's just a sprain." She explains.

"Why didn't you call me? I could have done it for you." I sweep her up in my arms, carrying her slight form to her sofa.

Why does she think she needs to do everything on her own?

"Don't be silly, Mac. I can do things like this myself." She waves away my worry like a pesky fly.

"I know you're fully capable of doing it yourself but that doesn't mean you need to do it alone." I stress my point while tamping down my irritation and hurt. "You can rely on me. That's what people in relationships do."

Even though we haven't had the relationship talk, we've been together exclusively these past couple of months.

A burning need suddenly bursts inside me, needing her to acknowledge what we are. Accept that I'm here for her.

"Mac, why are you getting upset? It's not a big deal." With another wave of her hand, she tries to avoid the conversation.

"Siren, it is a big deal. I know this is new to you but when you're in a relationship, you rely on your partner. If you can't even call me for help with something as simple as changing batteries, how am I supposed to trust that you'll come to me with the heavier stuff?" I'm voicing my biggest fear but she's worth the risk. I need her to be on the same page as me.

The hesitation on her face breaks my heart. Standing here like a dumbass, I watch as she withdraws from me. "Is that what we're doing? We're in a relationship?"

She doesn't get it.

I don't think as I cross the room. Cupping her face, I wait patiently for her eyes to connect with mine. She needs to get the seriousness of my words.

"Yes, baby. We're in a relationship. I want to be with you. I thought you wanted the same thing." The words scrape past my suddenly dry throat. Self-doubt plagues me as I watch her struggle to respond.

All my shortcomings flash through my mind, like a highlight reel of all the times I've let down the people that need me.

With a sense of dread, I watch hopelessly while she stares at me. The silence deafening, leaving me lost in swirling emerald pools as I await whatever fate will fall from her lips.

Foreboding is a tangible thing as I will her to say something. *Anything* to show me she's in this as deep as I am.

My heart breaks into a million pieces as the uncomfortable silence stretches.

She breaks it what feels like an eternity later. "I don't know. This is a lot to take in. I need some time."

With those simple words, she completes the shattering of the heart I didn't even realize I handed over to her. "You need time to think about us?"

"Yes. I need time." Averting her gaze, she doesn't see my heart fracturing in front of her. There is no way for me to hide the hurt in my eyes.

"Look at me, Siren." If she's going to shatter my world, the least she can do is meet it head on.

It takes her a minute but she finally brings those emerald orbs up to meet my heartbroken ones.

"I love you, Siren. This is what I want. I want to be with you. I'll give you some time to come to terms with that but I will be back."

With that promise, I turn to walk back out the door, leaving a part of my soul behind.

Chapter Thirty-Two

Kate

I'm numb.

I haven't moved.

I can't think.

I'm stuck on the couch, mind spinning since Mac left after dropping some serious bombs on me.

I have no idea how our conversation went so sideways.

How did you let that go so bad, so fast?

The walls are closing in on me. I've spread myself so thin trying to fit Mac into my life. Have I made a mistake? My life doesn't feel like it has room for a man right now.

But can you imagine your life without him?

I just don't know.

Hobbling my way to the kitchen, I grab a glass and a bottle of wine, pouring until the blood red liquid completely fills the glass.

Fear of abandonment rears its ugly head. I know it's an irrational fear. One I have no control over.

What if I'm not good enough? What if I give myself fully to him and he leaves the same as my mom? Lord knows, I never measured up to either of my parent's standards.

If I go all in and he walks away, Mac has the power to break me. And why would he stay? There are so many better options out there. In no way do I compare to other women he could have. The baggage I come with is heavy.

But the thought of him with another woman, a woman much more suitable to his lifestyle, brings on a fit of jealousy so strong, I almost throw my wine glass across the room.

The chime of my phone thankfully pulls me out of my downward spiral.

Jade: girl we r goin shoppin Saturday

Another message pops up before I can even respond.

Jade: Ur not gettin out of it

Ugh, she sure is relentless. It must be an MC thing. She could give Mac a run for his money in that department.

Just the thought of him brings me full circle. Right back to my dilemma.

Better respond to Jade before I head down that rabbit hole.

Me: Ok fine. We can go this weekend

If I don't give in, she'll keep pushing me. Might as well get this over with.

Maybe she'll change her mind when Mac tells her what happened today.

Glass of wine in hand, I shuffle down the hallway and collapse on my bed. Once I situate my foot on a pillow, I lean back and stare at the opposite wall.

Then I lay there contemplating my life and what could be with Mac, not sure I have the courage to reach out and grab the possibility.

***

Surprisingly, Jade didn't change her mind about our shopping trip so I'm rushing around my room to get ready.

I don't really have room in my schedule for this, taking time away from my volunteer schedule but Jade isn't taking no for an answer.

Believe me, I've tried.

Every time I try to reschedule, she insists I need this break from my busy life.

I'm conflicted.

Overwhelmed.

But everyone is encouraging me to take breaks and have some fun.

They say I need balance in my life.

Imagine that. People that actually care and want to be friends with you.

Ugh, there's no need to be so sarcastic.

And here I am arguing with myself now. This is what my life has devolved into.

We're meeting at Sweet Treats this morning. A necessary caffeine fix before heading to the mall in Redford. Frostown is too small to keep a mall in business. If you want to shop, you have to head out of town.

Mac isn't the only one who has gotten through my defenses. Demi has become my best friend. I'm still not quite sure how she snuck in but she's firmly entrenched herself in my soul.

I can't even remember what my life was like before that fateful day I walked through her doors.

I'm bummed she's not coming with us today. The experience just won't be the same without her.

Unfortunately, she's had no luck finding reliable help for the bakery. If you think she would let it get her down, you'd be wrong.

Her bubbly personality won't allow for that.

Pushing through the doors, I beeline straight to the counter where she already has my order waiting. She's been doing everything in her power to brighten my days since Mac upended my world.

Her smile is contagious, my lips spread in a more subdued one as I reach across the counter for a hug.

That's another new thing for me. Except with April, I have never been a touchy-feely person.

But Demi doesn't let me get away with that.

"Hey girl! You ready for your day out with the girls?" Her usual enthusiasm sounds loud and clear.

"Not like I really have a choice. I wish you were going with us."

"Girl, me too. I'm bummed I can't go with." Shrugging off her disappointment, nerves skitter down my spine at the deviousness of her smile. "But I hear Jade has plans for you."

"That's what I'm afraid of." And I am.

I have a strong feeling Jade is going to push me well out of my comfort zone today. It's no secret she wants to spice up my wardrobe.

Jade has an effortless sexiness that I envy. All the girls from the clubhouse do but Jade is the only one that doesn't make me feel inferior. Not to say the others have intentionally done so. There is just something about Jade draws me in.

Her happiness is genuine when I visit the clubhouse. It's not a front she puts on. Which is the only reason I'm giving her some leeway for this shopping trip.

"They're waiting for you at their regular table." Glancing over my shoulder, I see she's telling the truth.

I turn back to say goodbye, procrastinating a minute longer to give myself time to channel my inner voice before approaching the table of beautiful women.

"Alright, I'll see you tomorrow." I tell Demi.

She wants to hear all about today's shopping trip. So, I'm stopping by tomorrow to give her the details.

"Don't have too much fun without me!" Her wink lightens her command.

Still, I reach for her hand on the counter, giving it a squeeze. "You know it's not possible to have the best time without you."

She shoos me away with a grateful smile. The impatient customer behind me takes the opening to step to the counter.

Here goes nothing.

My inner voice is ready by the time I arrive at the table. "Good morning, ladies!"

Fake it til you make it, right?

Jade jumps from her chair, wrapping me in a fierce hug.

She's another tactile one.

"Good morning, Kate. We've been waiting forever! Are you ready? Do you want to finish your coffee first?" Her rapid-fire questions are infused with her excitement.

"Ready as I'll ever be. I can finish my coffee in the car." My words hold far less enthusiasm but Jade ignores it.

"Great. Let's roll out girls!" She yells out to the table of ladies while grabbing my hand.

"Jade, how much caffeine have you had?" I choke out through a laugh as she tows me out of the bakery.

"Silly, I'm excited! I never thought you'd let me take you shopping. I want to go before you change your mind!" Keeping my hand in hers, words rush out of her mouth as fast as her feet lead us out the door, stopping at an SUV parked on the street. Jade offered to drive when all the girls wanted to go with us but I had no idea it would be a luxury vehicle.

She glances at me over her shoulder at my faltering steps, then stops to give an explanation at the surprised look on my face. "It belongs to the club. Mac gave me the keys. He wouldn't take no for an answer when I mentioned we would need to take two cars."

Even after I pushed him away, he's intent on giving me the best experience with the girls.

It melts my heart.

His thoughtfulness has been evident in his every move during the past months.

I'm starting to believe he really wants me.

The girls chat the entire drive to Redford. Me? I'm sporting a perma-blush the whole time.

Their sexual escapades with the men of the club are unreal. They make no secret of the fact they love sex and are up for just about anything, anytime, anywhere.

Like Demi, there's no shame in their game.

There is just no way I will ever be as blasé about sex as these girls.

Despite the spell Mac weaves when I'm with him, I've managed to hold on to a sliver of sensibility when he's teased me in public.

He also doesn't push you too far. He respects your boundaries.

Interestingly, none of their stories mention Mac.

I'm drawn from my thoughts when Jade takes the exit for the mall in Redford.

I don't get out here much, so the growth in the area astonishes me. Stores now line both sides of the road to the mall.

Once we park, the girls pile out amidst excited chatter.

Moving at a slower pace, I trail them through the mall entrance, nerves running amok in my belly. Now that we're here, I'm a little apprehensive about giving Jade free rein to reinvent my wardrobe.

I move toward the department store I typically shop at but Jade is having none of that. She takes my hand and drags me right past the doors, not stopping until she finds an edgier store popular with my female students.

"I don't know, Jade. I don't think this is the right place for me."

She squeezes my hand to stop me when I try to return to the familiar department store, conveniently ignoring my protest. "Kate, come on. Give it a chance. Do you really think I'd do you wrong?"

I don't think that at all. She's been nothing but friendly and compassionate since I met her. It's my own insecurities causing my hesitation.

There is not a single thing in that store I would be comfortable in. But one look at her hopeful expression breaks me, my hesitation the opening she's looking for to drag me victoriously through the door.

Dropping my hand like a hot potato, she beelines to a display of flashy tops.

Definitely not something I would choose for myself.

My anxiety increases with each garment draped over her arm as she swipes through the selections. Tops of all shapes and colors I could never imagine myself wearing.

Despite her assurances that I'll look hot.

Or maybe *because* of them.

Moving on to skirts, she continues adding to the intimidating stack until her arms overflow.

With a pile of clothes as high as my anxiety, she somehow finds my hand again to lead me to a dressing room.

She's like a tornado whirling through the store.

And I am just along for the ride.

"Here we go. Try these on and don't forget we want to see you." Her order is delivered with a stern look.

"Okay." I give in with a roll of my eyes. I know when I'm facing a fiercer opponent than myself.

Grabbing the first item from the pile of intimidation, I hold up the tiniest skirt I have ever seen. Taking a deep breath – there is no way this will fit – I slip it up my legs until it settles on my hips, the material hugging my curves almost lovingly.

The reflection in the mirror promptly has me tugging down the scrap of material self-consciously. All that does is reveal my belly when the skirt slides down to cover more of my thighs.

Fearing Jade won't let me hide in here forever, I take a moment to fortify myself then quickly open the door.

Like ripping off a band-aid.

Catcalls and whistles echo off the walls when the girls catch sight of me.

"Kate, you look hot!" Raquel's delighted squeal comes from somewhere to my right.

I'm not so sure about that.

"I don't know. I don't think I can wear this." I contradict.

Jade moves to stand in front of me, her smile authentic. Pulling me over to the full-length mirror, she shifts behind me with her hands on my hips. "You know what I see when I see you in this outfit?"

"An old teacher trying to fit in with her students?" My attempt at humor falls flat as I watch her shake head in the reflection.

"No. I see a sexy woman. A woman who has one of the hottest, most loyal men I know tied up in knots. Because that is what you are, a sexy woman with a heart of gold. You have no idea how sexy you are. And that, my friend, is what makes you so irresistible."

Her words are like a balm to my soul. Never have I ever thought of myself that way.

Like that wasn't enough, her next words have me fighting tears. "Mac is my oldest friend. We've been through so much together. All I've ever wanted is to see him happy. I am so grateful he found you. You *are* the perfect woman for him."

Touched by the sincerity in her words, I refocus on my own reflection, taking a long critical look.

I let her words sink into my soul. It takes a minute but I finally see it.

I acknowledge her beautiful words with a smile. Allow myself to accept the veracity in her words.

I begin to see what others have tried to tell me.

The woman in the mirror is a gift.

The quintessential worth to her new friends. Not because she is perfect but because she's perfect for them.

"Okay, I'll take it." The moment is broken by the cheers of the girls behind us.

And that is how the rest of the afternoon goes. The girls drag me into store after store. Stores I never would have had the courage to step foot in before meeting Mac, Demi and the women and men of the MC.

They draw me in with jokes and laughter, continuing to shatter my defenses.

Not even caring about the hit to my wallet, I walk out of the mall with an entirely new wardrobe – and outlook.

But no money could possibly compare to the gift they've given me today.

These ladies have accepted me with an openness I could never have imagined the first time I met them.

Even Josie's hostility has lessened. I wouldn't say we'll ever be as close as I am with Demi and Jade, but I am happy to see the death glares have thawed. She's more like the pesky annoying sister I never had.

The same as Demi, I couldn't imagine my life without them.

Chapter Thirty-Three

Mac

It's been a week since Kate devastated my world. Seven days, I have wallowed in self-doubt.

Staring into the shot of whiskey on the bar in front of me, I lose myself to my dark thoughts. I'm not good enough for the hard times. The good time guy, not the long-term guy. Not the reliable guy.

The chirp of my phone pulls me from the darkness. April's name on the screen twists that darkness in another direction. I immediately imagine something horrible happened to Kate.

"April, what's wrong?" Panic laces my words.

"Hi Mac. I'm sorry to bother you but I didn't know who else to call. Kate was supposed to pick me up but she isn't here and she's not answering my calls." I hear the tears gathering in her voice.

My agitation mounts. Did something happen to her? Did DeLuca or Smith get their hands on her?

"When was the last time you heard from her?" I fight to keep some semblance of calm in my voice.

No need to freak April out too.

"We talked this morning before school. She said she had a couple people to help this afternoon." She says.

"Okay. Where are you?" I ask.

"At the library. I can walk home from here but Kate doesn't like me walking in the dark."

I didn't want that either. "No, don't walk home. I'll pick you up. Be there in ten."

"Thanks, Mac." She hangs up before I can tell her it's not a problem.

I stop in Byte's room before I leave. "Byte, I need you to track Kate's phone." I know it's an invasion of her privacy but that just is not my priority right now. "She was supposed to pick up April but she didn't show and she's not answering her phone." I explain while trying to keep my shit together.

If I had any doubts about my feelings for her, this situation really opens my eyes to what I truly want. "I'm going to pick up April. I'll see if she wants to come back here or go home. Text me what you find."

"You got it, man." He says, fingers already flying over his keyboard.

Jumping in the SUV, my mind races as fast as the vehicle as I fly down the road. April waits on the steps of the library when I pull up out front. She rushes up to the passenger side and flings open the door. "Thanks, Mac. I didn't know who else to call."

"It's no problem, April. I told you whatever you need, I'm here for both you and Kate. I'm glad you called me." And I mean it. The fact she turned to me for help means she is starting to trust me.

Maybe people do see me as reliable.

The problem is, the one person I want to rely on me just will not do it.

"Kate just called me. She said she lost track of time at Mr. Grayson's and her phone was on vibrate." That's a relief.

With that relief comes anger. "I don't know how many times I've told her that she needs to cut back all the hours she works. She's running herself ragged with everything she's trying to do."

In the ensuing silence, I worry that April will take my concern the wrong way. "Sorry, I'm not complaining about her work. I know it means a lot to her. I just think she overworks herself."

"No, you're fine." She assures me. "I'm worried too. I've tried talking to her about it. She doesn't want to hear that she needs to accept help."

"Yeah. That's it exactly. She was upset when I tried talking to her about it too."

I'm definitely not one to talk about my problems but April and me? We want the same thing. "Maybe if we both sit down with her, we'll get through to her."

The brightening of April's face gives me hope that we can make this work. "Do you think so?"

"April, I want this relationship to work with Kate. And that includes a relationship with you. I know we're not close to being a family but I hope we can get there some day." I've already laid myself bare to Kate and I want April to understand I am in this with both of them. "I want the best for both of you." We drive in silence for a few minutes. It's not uncomfortable, more like she's weighing my words. "What are you thinking?"

"I just want Kate to be happy. If that's with you, then that's what I want. I know I've been giving her a hard time lately but only because I was afraid she would leave me if she's with you. She's the only family I have left." She glances down like she's embarrassed to say it.

Probably wasn't planning to share all that with me.

I reach over to give her hand a quick squeeze. "April, you don't need to explain. I completely understand. Like I told you before, I'm here for you too and I want you both to be happy."

Chapter Thirty-Four

Kate

This last week has been a rollercoaster of emotions, swinging from the highest of highs to the lowest of lows.

I need a distraction, so decide to stop in the bakery for a much-needed chat with Demi.

Immediately sensing my melancholy, she drags me to our table for coffee and a decadent croissant. She then proceeds to regale me with the most outlandish recounting of setting up the bakery.

I snort through my laughter. My coffee almost spraying out my nostrils at the hilarious mishap Demi is currently describing. The scene plays out vividly in my mind courtesy of her attention to detail.

Her spellbinding stories have been pouring out since we sat down. I am transfixed by her outrageous misadventures. Crazy things that just do not happen to normal people.

I'm learning more about her life before we met, grateful she is finally opening up.

There is still one thing that is still off-limits. Her life in California. And the reason that really brought her here.

Baby steps.

"There is no way that happened!" Disbelief colors my voice.

I can do nothing but stare at her in bewilderment while ignoring the burn in my sinuses from my ill-timed drink.

Her stories are just too comical to believe.

"Girl, I'm telling you. It happened. I was stuck for over an hour before the movers came back." The ring of my phone interrupts us.

I glance down to see it's Mrs. Smith calling. She has become more than a client. She's the grandmother I wished for growing up.

I knew the first time we met we would grow close. Like so many of my clients, loneliness is the biggest challenge. Missing a family that is too busy to make time for her. A family that doesn't realize how precious that time really is.

Despite the story my coworker told me, I get the feeling they weren't as close as he led me to believe.

"Good afternoon, Mrs. Smith." I answer my phone. "How are you doing today?"

"Kate, I need your help." My smile turns to a frown at her words. "I fell out of my wheelchair and I'm not able to get up." I hear the tears she's holding back even through the phone.

Mouthing "emergency" to Demi, I stand from the table. She whispers to come back when I'm done.

I'm already out the door, focus back on Mrs. Smith, a burning need to get to her as fast as possible. "I'm on my way. Did you hurt yourself?"

"No, thank God. I just need help getting back into my chair. It's more embarrassing than anything." She says.

"Don't be embarrassed. We all need help from time to time. I'm getting in the car now. I'm on Main Street, so I should be there in about fifteen minutes."

"Be safe dear. I'll be fine until you get here." There's something off in her voice but I am so frantic I assume it's just the stress from her fall.

Ten minutes later, my car screeches to a stop in her driveway, probably losing some rubber on the asphalt too. Throwing the gear in park, I sprint up the walkway and use my key to open the door.

Now is not the time for knocking.

Chastising myself for not asking where in the house she fell, I call her name from the foyer. My feet pound the wood floors like a stampede of wild animals as I search for her.

"Mrs. Smith?" I try again when there's no response to my frantic yells.

My panic mounts as I come up empty in each room. The only sounds my heavy breathing and pounding heart. With no sign of her in the master bedroom or bathroom, I move back to the front of the eerily silent house.

Entering the kitchen, I stop short at the doorway when it's not Mrs. Smith I find.

Her nephew and a man I don't know stand there. Almost as if they were waiting for me.

Crap, Mac doesn't know I came here today.

"Michael, what are you doing here? Where is your aunt? She called me for help." Even I can hear the panic rising in my voice.

Instead of answering my question, he glances at the stranger. My attention swings his way too. "Kate, come in. Meet my friend Vince."

Who gives a crap about his friend?

"I'm here for your aunt. She needs help." I work hard to stay composed. Still so focused on Mrs. Smith, I don't think to question his presence here.

He crosses the kitchen with an ugly smirk, taking my arm in a firm grip. So lost in my panic about Mrs. Smith, my self-preservation is nowhere in sight.

My compliance allows him to drag me across the room to his friend. "Vince and I have some questions for you."

"What are you talking about, Michael?" I play up the confusion. There is no way they know for sure that I'm helping the MC. "I don't even know who he is. What questions could I possibly answer?"

"You might not know him, but he knows who you are. More importantly, he knows who you spend your time with." Michael says. The stranger remains eerily silent.

Finally taking a closer look at this Vince guy, I *did not* like the way he was watching me.

My self-preservation finally kicks in at the creepy look on his face. I struggle to pull away but Michael's hold on my arm doesn't let me get far, really only serving to tighten his grip. His biting fingers dig into my bicep.

Trying a different tactic, I relax my muscles and soften my tone.

"Michael, you're hurting me." Maybe a heavy dose of meekness will sway him.

"Your boyfriend's club took something from me and I want it back." Vince speaks for the first time.

The only thing Mac's club took was his family.

I'll be damned if I let him anywhere near them.

Really hoping I'm a halfway decent actress, I infuse my voice with confusion.

"What are you talking about? I don't know anything about Mac's club."

"We know you don't. You're the bait to get back what I want." Well, at least they don't know I've been trying to help the club.

But then the implication of his words registers.

My dire situation really sinking in.

"What are you going to do to me?" This time the fear in my voice is real. Chills slither down my spine at the realization that I am stuck in this house alone with these men.

From the lascivious look in Vince's eyes, I'm not sure I want his answer, so I turn my gaze to Michael.

"You and I are going for a little ride." He says. "Vince has one last thing to take care of before he meets us there."

Too late, my flight instincts scream at me to run just as Michael's fist flies at my face.

Crap. If we leave this house, it will be that much harder for someone to find me.

And that's my last thought before my vision goes black.

Chapter Thirty-Five

Mac

You would think Joker's mood would be lighter now that we have Sarah set up in the clubhouse – and away from her dirtbag husband.

You'd think wrong. If anything, it has only gotten worse. A dark storm brews in his eyes.

He is spoiling for a fight. A fight he's about to get it if he doesn't back off Bomber.

I have no clue what they're even arguing about.

He is on his own if he's willing to put his life on the line with the serious brother.

Looks like the rest of my brothers are of the same thought. No one is stepping in to stop the bomb that is Bomber about to explode.

Tuning them out, I check my phone again. Kate still hasn't answered my last text.

A burning need grows inside me. To lay eyes in her. To hold her. To talk to her. She's had enough space. Enough time. It's about time I get my woman back.

Ryker's approach saves me from sending my millionth text. Setting my phone on the bar, I wait impatiently for whatever he has to say.

"Hey man. Wanted to give you a heads up. We'll take it to vote tonight to approach Kate about setting up that shelter at the abandoned hotel down the road." He says. "It's not the best option having a mother and her children hiding out at the clubhouse. If we're gonna go this route, we need to put this shit in motion. Do you think she'll be receptive to the idea?"

The thing about my girl – her heart is huge. No way she'll turn her back if there is any way she can help people in need. That's obvious in the joy that lights her up when she talks about her clients. She could go on for days.

"I don't see a downside for her. And knowing how much she wants to make a difference in the community, I don't think she'll be able to say no." My words seem to lift a huge weight off his shoulders. All that's left to do now is take it to a vote with the club.

Prez has never steered us wrong. Everyone here trusts him with their life. If he's convinced this is the best way to make a difference in the local community, we are all in a hundred percent.

"Thanks man. Was hoping to hear that." He turns to head to the back of the clubhouse.

Leaving me to stew in my thoughts again. I'm doing my best not to worry that Kate is ghosting me.

I'm powerless to stop myself from sending one more text. My fingers freezing on the screen when Demi races through the clubhouse door.

Cold hard dread fills me. Slithers of fear a desperate dance down my spine.

Because Kate is nowhere in sight.

The fact Demi is supposed to be with Kate – and obviously isn't – my blood turns to ice. The look on her face says it all.

Something is wrong.

Ryker pivots to intercept her at the door. "Demi, what are you doing here? What's wrong?"

Prez feels it too.

Demi ignores him. Instead, sidestepping him to cross the room to me. "Mac, I think something happened to Kate."

"What do you mean? I thought she was with you." I do my best to keep panic at bay.

Newsflash, it doesn't work one bit.

"She was at the bakery earlier but she got a call from Mrs. Smith. Then she ran out. From what I could hear, she fell or something and needed Kate's help. Before she left, I told her to come back when she was done. When she didn't respond to my texts, I tried calling her but she's not answering. Now her phone is going straight to voicemail and I haven't seen her." Breathless after her word vomit, Demi finally stops to refill her lungs before continuing.

"I'm worried about her. I know I'm a lot to take but she has *never* ignored me before. Even when she's super busy, she still responds to let me know she'll get back to me later. I just have a feeling something bad happened."

A fear I have never felt before seizes my mind, shivering down my spine once again at the mention of Mrs. Smith. Of an emergency at her house. It all seems too convenient.

Despite the many life or death situations I've been in – both in my military career and with the club – this is completely different. My soul fractures. Just the thought of something happening. Of Kate scared. Alone.

All because I was a coward. Too scared of a second rejection to grow some balls and confront her about us. Because there is an *us*.

And now we may never get that chance.

"How long ago did she leave the bakery?" Byte questions.

I completely forgot the others were even in the room, helplessness a living beast inside me.

Thankfully, Byte understands my fear without a word. Recognizes my symptoms. Gives me this moment to collect myself.

He's listened to all of my worries about Kate getting close to Smith's aunt.

"She left three hours ago. She should've at least let me know if she couldn't get back to the bakery." Demi says.

She's right. Kate wouldn't want her friend to worry about either Mrs. Smith or herself.

"Byte, look into Smith again. Check the aunt's records too. Phone, financials, properties, everything." Ryker takes charge. Barking out orders.

Byte is already sprinting back to his room to get started.

"Ryker?" Demi's voice cuts through my whirling thoughts. So caught in my mental paralysis, I completely forgot she was there.

I drop into the closest chair, unsteady legs no longer able to hold me up.

Knowing me well, Ryker's hand falls on my shoulder. It gives me the strength to clear the haze. I do my best to refocus on my brother.

Get your shit together, asshole.

I need to be strong for my girl.

"We'll find her brother." He assures me.

Josie appears from the kitchen. And obviously senses something happened. "What's wrong?"

"Who's this 'Smith' person? Do you think someone took Kate?" Demi's scared voice reverberates throughout the room.

Ryker makes another move to steer her out of the clubhouse but she's not having any of that.

Fearless, Demi gets right in his face. "Answer me, Ryker! Do you think something happened to Kate?" Her voice piercing as she loses her shit.

Obviously at the end of his patience, Ryker bends to plant his shoulder in her stomach. He straightens with her in a fireman's carry.

His stomping feet are drowned out by her cries as they disappear down the hallway. The sounds suddenly cut off with the slam of his office door.

Well shit. That isn't good.

With the show over, Bomber answers Josie's question. "Kate is missing."

If I wasn't watching Josie so closely, I would have missed the flinch on her face. The guilt she can't hide.

"Do you know something Josie?" It's unfathomable that she does but I will turn over every stone to find my girl.

"Mac. I didn't know who he was when I first met him." She says.

"What are you talking about Josie? Met who?" Bomber interjects.

Shame steals over her face. "DeLuca. He approached me at a bar. Introduced himself as "Vince" but I swear I didn't know who he was. I was already drunk when I started talking to him. I was hurt and I vented about you and Kate hooking up."

"So, you set her up? Do you know what kind of people we're dealing with? You saw what he did to Sarah when we brought her to the clubhouse." I roar. Fury doesn't even begin to describe how I feel in this moment.

I can't even look at her. "Get her out of my sight. We need to talk to Prez." The sight of her disgusts me.

The stunned silence doesn't last long. Byte's pounding feet momentarily distract me from Josie's confession.

"I think I might know where she is. Mac, you know the teacher hooked Kate up with his aunt?" I push down my hope. But it's hard to do with the excitement in his voice.

"Yes. Do you have something?" Doing my best to keep my shit together, I want to shake him. Force him to spill faster. Whatever news he has is better than nothing. We need every piece of intel to find my girl.

"I looked deeper into the aunt. She lives in the house she bought with her husband when they were married. She also has a cabin near Redford that she hasn't been to in years. It was passed down through the husband's family, so it didn't show up in my initial background check. I think, with her health issues, she physically wouldn't be able to get up there."

He rolls on. "I hacked the power company. There was no activity until about three months ago. Then the usage spiked and has stayed steady ever since."

"With his connection to the teacher, my money is on dumbass Vinny needing a place to hide out." Rocker says. "We aren't the only ones interested in his whereabouts."

A burst of anticipation expels me from my chair. I'm at the door before any of the brothers can stop me. "Send me the address. I'm going up there."

"Brother, we need a plan. Don't go up there half-cocked. All that's gonna do is get someone hurt and you don't want that person to be Kate." Byte's logic – usually appreciated – just pisses me off now.

The terror inside me won't tolerate a delay. It's a compelling need to get to Kate as swiftly as humanly possible. A fervent impulse to protect my woman.

Rocker, the big ass motherfucker, steps in front of me. Arms crossed, no words necessary to halt me in my tracks.

Joker takes the opportunity to slip down the hallway to bang on Ryker's door. "Prez! We got a lead."

Stomping back in the main room, the anger on Joker's face is clear. I don't need anyone to tell me the same is reflected on mine.

In less than thirty seconds, Ryker comes out of his room alone. Hair disheveled, scowl in place. All the brothers know better than to take their lives in their hands to ask what the hell happened back there.

"What did you find?" He demands.

Byte brings him up to speed on the cabin and the assumption DeLuca has been staying there. And Josie's role in all of it.

"Good job, brother." He responds to Byte with angry eyes on a trembling Josie.

A beat of silence passes before Ryker throws out more orders – completely ignoring the blatantly nosy looks from all the brothers.

"Joker, you stay here with Demi and Josie. Guard Sarah and the kids. Make sure none of them leave. Byte, keep digging into both the teacher and the trucker. They'd be idiots to go somewhere connected to either of them but we'll head out there to check for sure. See if you can get eyes on the place. Everyone else, let's roll out."

Finally given the order for action, I race out the door to get to my woman. *I just pray we're not too late.*

Chapter Thirty-Six

Kate

The throbbing in my cheek rudely pulls me from darkness.

Michael's fist sure packed a punch – pun intended.

Slitting my eyes open, I survey my surroundings. It is immediately clear I'm in an unfamiliar house, nothing here recognizable.

Girl, you're not at Mrs. Smith's house anymore.

Movement in my periphery catches my attention. I tilt my head slightly to the left to see Michael pacing in the next room.

It seems to be a cabin but I can't tell for sure from my limited view.

Unfortunately, my movement is enough to draw Michael's attention. His pacing footsteps halt as he turns to fully face me.

"Oh good, you're awake. I thought I seriously hurt you." He almost sounds disappointed.

My jaw would disagree. It feels like a wrecking ball slammed into it.

"Where are we?" I keep my voice faint. It might be helpful to play up the injury. Maybe lower his guard in case I can find an opportunity for escape.

But then feeling returns to my limbs and I realize I can't move my arms. The ropes around my wrists are hard to miss when I glance down.

Well crap. So much for making my escape.

Looks like I'm stuck for now. Might as well push for answers. "Michael, answer me. Where are we?"

He waves my question away. "Where we are doesn't matter. Where did the club take Vince's wife and kids?" His continued avoidance of my questions is frustrating.

I need to play up my confusion. I won't let them find Sarah and the kids.

Trying not to draw his attention, I test the tightness of the ropes with no luck. Tied securely to the arms of the chair, I'm not going anywhere unless he unties me. Something tells me that isn't going to happen.

Fear eats at me. Fear that I may never see April or Mac again. If only I'd listened to Mac. Asked for help instead of trying to take on the world by myself. If I had just talked to him. If I let him know when Mrs. Smith called.

Told him I love him.

My fingers clench as I fight the panic now threatening to overtake me. The what if's consuming.

Get yourself together.

Time to see how good my acting skills really are. I need to find a way out of this crappy predicament. If he's talking, he's not taking action and I need to take advantage of his chattiness to buy myself some time.

No one knows where I am. I need to figure out a way to save myself. Because of my stupid stubbornness nobody else is going to do it.

Mac was right, I can't do it all myself.

Now I just need to survive long enough to tell him he was right.

"I have no idea, Michael. I don't even know Vince. How would I know anything about his wife and kids? Are they in danger?"

He's clearly delusional and that doesn't bode well for me. I really don't want to be here when Vince shows up.

Maybe a show of concern for Vince's family will win me some brownie points.

"The only danger they're gonna be in is when Vince finds them. He hid cash in one of his son's toys. We need that money to disappear." Well crap, there goes that idea.

What a douchebag. Hiding cash in his kids toys.

My thoughts must reflect on my face.

"You want to judge? How about you judge your man?" Air quotes accompany the word man. He's jumping subjects so fast he's giving me whiplash.

"A little birdie told us he only got close to you for their investigation."

Little does he know I pushed my way into their investigation.

Focus girl. You need to get yourself out of this crappy situation. You won't get the chance to confess your love to Mac if you don't make it out of here alive.

I steal my spine and keep him talking. "So, if that's the case, the MC isn't going to take the bait. Why would they care what happens to me?"

"Because even if he is only using you, that bunch of do-gooders can't help themselves. They have to ride in to save the day." Mouth practically foaming, spittle flies as his voice rises. "They should have kept their nosy asses out of it! We had a good thing going until they got involved." He roars.

"Michael, I already told you I have no idea what you're talking about. You need to let me go." I sound like a broken record. And I don't think he's buying it.

Why did you have to be so stubborn?

And how the heck are you going to get out of this?

Chapter Thirty-Seven

Mac

Riding hell-bent for leather, we make it to Redford in thirty minutes instead of the usual hour.

If we passed any cops, there was no way they would have caught us.

Signaling from the front, Ryker slows the brothers to a stop on the outskirts of town.

"Byte said the cabin is too isolated for digital surveillance but he connected with an old friend to hike up there to check it for us. He reported back ten minutes ago. There's one vehicle out front, fits the description of the teacher's SUV." I wait impatiently for more intel. "There's movement inside the cabin. Looks like one male and one female present."

"Did he get a look at the woman? Is it Kate?" I have to know.

"The woman fits her description. She appeared to be unconscious but he didn't see any other signs of injury."

There's some relief at the news but my fear will not release its stranglehold on my heart until I have her in my arms. Unwilling to consider any other outcome, the only acceptable possibility to find her safe and unharmed.

Hang on, baby. We're coming for you.

She's unwittingly burrowed her way under my defenses until it was too late to do anything about it. She's so deeply ingrained in my DNA – losing her will kill me.

My life will be worthless without her.

"Bomber, the cabin is five minutes from here. I want you to go in ahead of the team." Ryker commands. "You have a clean shot, you take him out but only if there is no threat to Mac's old lady."

As a former sniper in the Navy, Bomber is the most skilled brother for the job.

While most of the original members crossed paths at some point in our careers, Ryker and Bomber served together the longest.

More than anyone, he knows Bomber is the calmest under pressure.

If there's a way to take out Smith without harming Kate, Bomb is the one I trust to get it done.

He'll give his own life to save my woman if it comes down to it.

Until I can get to her, my Siren will be in the best hands possible once Bomb has eyes on her.

The next ten minutes feel like an eternity, waiting for word from him.

Recognizing my need for space, all the brothers stand around their bikes. Their eyes track my pacing footsteps back and forth across the parking lot.

My heart feels like it's going to beat out of my chest while we wait.

What feels like an eternity later, but probably only five minutes at most, Ryker's phone sounds with a text. The only thing stopping me from ripping the damn thing out of his hand is the respect I have for him.

He's handling this situation like a military mission with a clear-headedness I'm currently incapable of.

There's no doubt in my mind that his leadership will get us through this mission successfully.

My heart won't let me believe any different.

"We're clear to roll out. Bomber confirmed it is your woman at the cabin. Smith is with her but no sign of DeLuca." He issues the update at the same time he mounts his bike. "Byte's friend is a medic. Now that we have a confirmed sighting, he has cops and EMTs on standby."

Rocker's slap to my back is the kick in the ass I need to get moving. A quick squeeze of his hand conveys his compassion before he follows Prez's lead.

"We'll get her, brother. Keep your head straight, don't let the bad shit stray you from your mission here." A man of few words, the forceful impact of his conviction stronger than a gut punch.

We head further up the mountain, riding in formation with Ryker leading the way. We only travel up the mountain road a few short minutes before he slows to a stop in a small clearing.

He points to a narrow path in the trees as he shuts down the engine and climbs off. "Bomb sent me the coordinates. We're going up this way. The path will lead us right to the backdoor of the cabin. Bomb has the front covered."

Guns in hand, we enter the forest of trees. On silent footsteps we move as a unit, making our way through the forest.

Ryker's raised fist stops us when we catch sight of the cabin at the edge of the clearing. All of us follow his lead as he changes direction, moving to the right until the cabin's back door comes into view.

It's all I can do to keep myself from breaking down the door and shooting the fucker that thought he could take what's mine.

Knowing my brothers have a plan – and my back – is the only thing stopping me when my instincts are screaming to storm the building to find my woman.

Ryker silently leads us to the back door of the cabin.

We stop short when voices sound from inside. I find some consolation recognizing Kate is one of them but it's too muffled to hear her clearly.

Smith's booming accusation suddenly comes through loud and clear. "They should have kept their nosy asses out of it! We had a good thing going until they got involved."

Shit, this is what I was afraid of.

"Michael, I already told you I have no idea what you're talking about. You need to let me go."

It takes a bear hug from Ryker to keep me from breaking down the door to get to my woman when her wavering words come through louder.

"Brother, I need you focused. Bomb said there's a figure pacing back and forth at the front windows. He's positive it's Smith. From the sound of Kate's voice, she's closer to us.

"We're going to create a distraction back here so Bomb can enter the front to take him down. You need to step back and let us handle this. We'll get your woman back safe."

I know he's right. I'm too caught up in my feelings. I need to take a breather and get my head on straight for Kate. She doesn't need me losing my shit, I need to stay calm for her.

Inhaling deep, I do just that. I step back from the door and take a minute to compose myself using the breathing techniques I learned from my recovery, when the pain in my shoulder was so bad it was a distraction from everything else around me.

I want to be worthy. I want it so bad I can taste.

It's that want. That desire to be worthy of her, my Siren, that finally has the power to calm my racing heart. Allows my mind to clear.

Once he sees I have my shit locked down, Ryker moves to stand in front of the door.

"Bomb, we're ready at the back door." He must have Bomber on the phone. Speaking through the earbud in his ear.

That's my last thought before we hear a commotion from the front, the sound of Bomb breaking through the front door.

Ryker wastes no time in taking action from the back. Throwing himself at the door, the frame crumbles under his full weight. Hinges groan, wood splinters, the door hanging on by a thread as he muscles his way in from the back.

Where am I? You can bet your ass I'm right on his heels.

My eyes take in the scene as soon as I step through the doorway. Relief immediate when I lay eyes on my woman at the kitchen table.

Bruised.

Tied to a fucking chair.

The beast inside me roars.

Chapter Thirty-Eight

Kate

An explosion from the front of the cabin catches Michael by surprise, cutting off his latest rambling insanity as he swings to face the unknown adversary. He does a one-eighty at the sounds of the door splintering behind me. The explosion of wood accompanying the thunderous pounding of several pairs of boots announce the men of the MC storming in like the cavalry.

Ryker might be leading the way but the next man through the door captures all my attention. Mac is right on his heels, zeroing in on me at once, my eyes ensnared by his intensity. Even through the grunting sounds of flesh hitting flesh, I see nothing but him.

He's an avenging warrior come to rescue the damsel.

And let's face it, that's exactly what this is.

"Siren." The emotion in his voice unleashes the tight reins on my emotions.

The waterworks I've held back release like a tidal wave as he drops down in front of me. I'm stuck in this stupid chair, unable to move when every fiber of my being aches to jump into his arms.

Unaware of the frantic thoughts racing through my head, he quickly gets to work on the ropes holding me immobile.

Despite the venom Michael tried to shove in my face – the face Mac is tenderly holding in place for his kiss – I can't contain my joy in this moment.

I knew in my gut Mac would come for me.

"Mac, get her out of here. Bomb subdued the teacher at the front. The sheriff is taking him into custody." Ryker's orders are the motivation Mac needs to turn back to untying my binds. Before they even hit the ground, he sweeps me up in his arms, rushing back out the door as quickly as he appeared.

"Mac, we have to get back to Mrs. Smith's house! I think they hurt her." I try to stop him.

"Baby, she's fine. We sent a prospect to her house when Demi told us you went there. He found her tied up in the closet but otherwise she's okay." With that assurance, the last of my fears melt away, leaving me boneless in his arms. Relieved the ordeal is over.

Even though Mac saved me, a newfound confidence soars. I kept myself together. I knew in my heart Mac would find me. Come for me. Save me.

I had the courage to do what I needed to do to survive.

***

Everything after Mac carried me out of that cabin is a blur. The EMT checking me over. The sheriff questioning me. Mounting Mac's motorcycle.

An eternity later, we're finally heading home. I cling to Mac as he flies down the highway, grateful for this second chance.

Grateful for the feel of his body so close to mine.

Grateful to experience the power of the machine beneath us, the way this amazing man handles the beast.

Pulling into my driveway, he doesn't say anything as he helps me off the motorcycle. His hold most gentle when he picks me up and moves silently up the porch steps where Demi stands like a sentinel on my porch.

"Mac wait. Michael said something weird when I was with him. He seemed to know things about the club. Things he shouldn't have. He said a 'little birdie' told him about your investigation."

The stoicism on his face, the hardness of his stare, it's as if he's distancing himself from me.

I cling tighter to his neck. "Mac, what's wrong?"

He ignores my question, instead moving his gaze to watch his step, carefully maneuvering up the steps of my front porch.

"Siren, I failed you. You never should've been left alone at Mrs. Smith's house." Jaw rigid, his gruff words tear from deep inside. Grating and ravaged, they tell the story of his fear.

Fear of losing me.

I feel cherished in this moment. This man who would give his life for mine.

My hand slides around his neck to cup his hair roughened jaw of its own accord, pulling his face down until our eyes meet. "Mac, you didn't fail me. You saved me when it counted. I never should have gone there on my own. I put myself at risk. This wasn't your fault."

My fingers rub softly back and forth over the softness of his beard. Soothing. Comforting.

His hold is gentle as he sets me on the couch. He breaks eye contact, moving away before speaking, his words directed to the wall above my head. "I should have been there, Kate. I failed you."

While I struggle for the words to convince him otherwise, Demi breaks our silent stare down. Well, my silent stare down since Mac still won't look away from the wall.

My best friend is a whirlwind of activity, bustling around Mac doing his best impersonation of a statue in the middle of my living room. She barks out orders with the confidence of a drill sergeant while fluffing the pillows on the couch.

"Demi-" I try to reassure her I am okay but she cuts me off.

"Don't you 'Demi' me, Kate. I almost lost my best friend. You need to let me take care of you."

Struck by the ferocity of her words, I don't even notice Mac's disappearance until Demi crouches down in front of me. The concerned look on her face causes me more anxiety than my kidnapping, distracting me from the loss of the man I love.

Demi isn't an emotional person, so to say I'm shocked by this display is an understatement.

"Come on, Sweetie. Let's get you to your room." Mouth clamped shut, I let her lead me to the shower, the water raining down like a cleansing for my soul.

What feels like a lifetime later, I step out to find my comfiest pajamas sitting on the counter. Utterly exhausted, I allow Demi to tuck me into bed for a much needed nap.

I'm numb.

That's probably for the best. I don't have the mental capacity to process everything that happened today.

I recognize the feeling, but I can't for the life of me figure out which emotion to focus on. My heart breaking from Mac's withdrawal, being personally acquainted with a drug dealer, or being taken hostage because I involved myself in the club's investigation into said drug dealer.

Take your pick. All of it too much for me to handle in this moment.

It was all I could do to get showered and dressed, asleep as soon as my head hit my pillow.

Chapter Thirty-Nine

Kate

My mental paralysis gives Demi the perfect opportunity to take over my life.

I don't argue.

That first night when Mac brought me home, I couldn't even make the simplest decisions.

She's patient. As patient as Demi can possibly be. She gives me exactly three days to dwell in my thoughts.

I'd be listening to an hour-long lecture if she realized giving me that time led to my decision to give Mac a chance to, at the very least, explain his actions the day he disappeared.

He let me past his hard exterior, showing me the tender and caring man beneath. The warmth, gentleness, compassion – I could keep going – those emotions were genuine. The way we came together, our bodies in perfect synchrony, there is no way to fake that.

Just the thought of him playing my body so perfectly spikes my arousal. It's been way too long since his skin touched mine, way too long since I felt him move inside me, stretching me just past the point of pain, taking me to heights of pleasure I never dreamed were possible.

There's a connection between us that I believe in.

I may have been an idiot to deny it, but I've smartened up. The time we've spent together has become a bond that tethers us.

I have no intention of walking away from this once in a lifetime connection.

At least not without answers.

If I'm wrong – if he no longer wants me – I'll leave him be. But if he feels the same, then this is something worth fighting for.

We are worth fighting for.

I will no longer let fear and shyness rule me. It's time I took that chance that kept me from living my life the way I always dreamed of. Hopefully, with Mac by my side.

Try as she might, Demi hasn't kept me completely isolated. Ryker has sweet talked – or maybe bulldozed – his way past her blockade a couple times.

The first time to check on me and assure us there wouldn't be any more threats against me. On his second visit, he blew my mind with an offer too good to be true.

I'm dumbfounded.

The MC wants to invest in me. Well, in a business with me, but one that I would have sole control over.

With one requirement. I set up and run a shelter for people escaping unsafe situations. A safe haven for those desperate to escape violence and hopelessness. In exchange, I'll be able to continue to volunteer my services in the community exactly as I always dreamed.

The plus side – I would no longer be limited to working around my job at the high school. The MC would fund my efforts.

Ryker explained that since their move to Frostown, the men have been looking for a way to contribute to the community. And they all believe this will be a meaningful investment. In both the town and me. Their faith in me adds another layer to a confidence that grows stronger by the day.

If there's a downside to saying yes, I haven't found it.

The MC already put in an offer on the abandoned hotel half a mile from the clubhouse. It's the perfect location for their vision.

All I have to do is say yes.

It's impossible to miss Demi's displeasure when Ryker stops by. Those visits end with Demi cursing him out the door.

Secretly, I think she feels threatened by what could be with that man. He makes no secret of his desire for her.

He seems up to the challenge that is my best friend.

Even though the blame for my involvement lies entirely with Michael, she disagrees. In her mind, I never would have been in danger if Mac hadn't gotten involved with me.

Spending the better part of the week talking her off the ledge after Ryker's visits, I put my foot down when she balked at my request to go to the clubhouse.

I know her hardheadedness is a byproduct of her fear of losing me but my conversation with Mac is long overdue. My friend is not going to stand in the way.

I'm dressed for battle in a black leather mini skirt, paired with an off the shoulder silky blouse. I even left my hair down for this.

In a war to win back my man, I will use whatever advantage possible, play as dirty as I must.

I'm in the middle of convincing my friend to drive me to the clubhouse.

"Absolutely not! They're the whole reason you were in danger in the first place!"

"Please Demi. I just want to talk to him. How am I supposed to get closure if I don't have this conversation with him?" I ask.

I've learned there are things worth fighting for and my shyness will not hold me back any longer.

I also wasn't above trickery. She has taught me well and I have guilt using her skills against her.

Let's see how much the master likes to be duped.

It takes some time but she finally relents in the face of my unwavering composure. Though she wouldn't be Demi if she didn't show her displeasure as she stomps out to the car.

Displeasure is too tame a word.

She is pissed.

I think this is the first time she has *ever* given someone the silent treatment. Her personality is too loud for that.

The only other time she's deigned to let me out of the house was when I demanded to see Mrs. Smith.

Even though Ryker assured me she was fine, I needed to know the ordeal didn't leave a lasting impression. I had an overpowering need to set eyes on her myself to put my mind at ease.

If Mr. Grayson was the grandfather I wished I had, Mrs. Smith is my vision of the quintessential grandmother.

Drawn out of my musings as we pull to a stop in front of the clubhouse, my sides expand on a deep breath before gripping the handle and stepping from the car.

I smooth down my shirt and face the clubhouse doors with one final thought.

It's time to get my man back.

Chapter Forty

Mac

It's been a fuck of a long week since everything went down at the cabin. The cops took Smith into custody after we found Kate. He's currently being held without bail pending multiple manslaughter and drug running charges.

DeLuca and Josie are in the wind. Byte has been glued to his computer to find them. The craziness of that day gave Josie the opportunity to slip past Byte and Joker. They're both kicking their own asses for allowing that to happen.

All the brothers want them to answer for their crimes.

Smith used his aunt to get to Kate. We were all relieved to find her alive and well. Albeit tied up in a closet after her nephew forced her to make that fateful call to lure Kate to his trap.

Like a fool, I abandoned Kate that night, letting my fear paralyze me at the memory of her tied to that chair. A mistake I'm still attempting to remedy.

When I came to my senses, it was too late. Demi took guard over my girl and hasn't stood down since.

No one needed to tell me I fucked up. I broke her friend's heart that night.

While I appreciate her dedication to protecting Kate, I am desperate to get to my girl. But Demi has blocked every attempt I've made to contact her. The door goes unanswered, the phone calls screened, and the tone of the texts tell me Demi has taken control there too.

My only consolation is the updates I get from Ryker.

I know Prez approached Kate about investing in her dream. The club unanimously voted to provide the funding for her to open a shelter to help those in need. The investment will allow Kate to focus on her true passion. She'll have the opportunity to help even more people in the community.

So far, she hasn't given him an answer. I'm positive it's only a matter of time until she agrees. Her passion just isn't in teaching. Even a blind person could see the way she lights up talking about the people she helps.

She's built a unique bond with each and every person we spoke to, the type of family she always wanted and she didn't even realize it. Non-traditional as it may be, they all love her.

Although this is an unconventional business combination, it's important to me to make my girl's dual dreams come true.

Hopefully with me at her side.

The abandoned hotel half a mile from the clubhouse is the perfect location to set up.

We won't proceed until she gives Ryker an answer. Other than putting in an offer on the place, we're at a standstill. This doesn't work without my girl running the show.

At a loss as to how to get my girl, I took a ride to see the Baker's in an attempt to take my mind off my problems.

We were finally able to give them the assurance they needed – the drug dealing in the area is done.

Not that it will ever replace what they lost, no parents should have to bury their child. I just have to believe it gives them enough peace to truly lay their son to rest.

Their warm greeting was a stark contrast to my first visit. I spent hours with them looking through picture after picture. Photo albums documenting the life lost so young. Jean and Marc were desperate to share happy memories of the son they lost way too soon.

Staring into my warm beer, I contemplate my next move. The clubhouse doors open behind me but I have no interest in any of the women the men brought back tonight.

That all changes when Demi's loud voice echoes through the clubhouse.

"I told you he was pathetic. Drinking at the bar alone? Girl, you can do so much better than this." Her sarcasm comes through loud and clear.

Sitting there like the pathetic ass she just accused me of, I can do nothing but drink in the sight of my girl as she saunters toward the bar with a serene confidence.

"Siren." One gritty word is all I am capable of in this moment.

Good job dumbass. You've waited a week to pour your heart out and that's all you got?

"Hi Mac." Her smile is tentative, almost like she's unsure of my reaction.

Who could blame her? You have no one to blame but yourself for that.

Her hair falls around her in a riot of sexy curls, springing back in place even as she shoves it behind her ear. I'm dying to bury my fingers in the mass, to get lost in the deceptive softness.

As she straightens her spine her shirt falls off one shoulder, giving me teasing glimpses of her cleavage. The sexy barely there leather skirt I want to slip my hands under. Find out what kind of panties the skirt hides. If any at all.

The vision of my Siren, sexily at ease in her newfound confidence, holds me captivated. My dick hard at the vision in front of me.

Deciding to step right into the deep end, I throw myself at her mercy, dying to know what her presence here means for me.

"What are you doing here? I didn't think you wanted to see me. You avoided me the last week." I know I sound like a fool but there's no stopping this train wreck.

Throwing her friend a glare, she returns her beautiful eyes to mine and takes a step closer. My hands itch to draw her closer, but she teasingly stops just out of reach.

"I just needed some time to think. That was a lot to take in and I needed to wrap my head around the whole situation." Before I have the chance to interject with an apology, she rolls right on.

"I only needed the first part of the week for that." She takes pity on me at the confusion I can't hide. "The rest of the time was spent keeping Demi from storming the clubhouse. She's a warrior when one of her own is threatened and for some reason she's decided that includes me."

Ignoring her attempt at humor, I hold her gaze with my intensity. I need her to understand the depth of my pride in her. Pride not only in how she handled her kidnapping but also her courage in coming here to confront me.

"Siren, the only warrior I see is you. You didn't lose your shit when you got caught up in the middle of our investigation. Even tied to that chair, you stood your ground and didn't let the fear overwhelm you."

From the look on her face, I have hope she is starting to believe me. My words penetrating her doubt in us, the protective walls around her heart crumbling.

Closing the distance between us, she steps into her rightful space between my legs before raising her eyes to mine again. "Mac, why did you choose me?"

This is the part where I have to lay it all on the line. Show my vulnerability if I want the future that is so close I can taste it. My life isn't worth a damn thing without my Siren by my side.

"Siren, it was never a choice for me. You embedded yourself so far into my soul, I couldn't separate us if I tried."

Her courage in entering the clubhouse – in confronting her fears – gives me the fortitude to continue.

"I love you, Siren. I want to entwine our lives until I don't know where you end and I begin. I want all my sunsets with you. I want all my sunrises to start with you in my arms. Approaching you was the best, and easiest, decision I've ever made in my life."

The pensive look she attempts does nothing to mask the combination of desire, mischief and love in her eyes.

It gives me hope.

"I don't know, Mac. Why don't you take me to bed and give me a preview of how entwined we can get?" I'm moving before she even finishes her question.

Picking her up bridal style, her arms wrap around my neck before I even take the first step.

"And Mac, just one more thing." She waits until my eyes are once again on hers before rocking my world.

"I love you too."

Thank fuck.

Chapter Forty-One

Kate

"Let's go." He doesn't wait for a response. Instead, he hauls off down the hallway to his room. It's a good thing he's carrying me. There is no way I could keep up with his hurried strides.

He drops my legs to the floor as soon as the door slams behind us, pressing me up against the hard wood, his strong body holding me in place. Forearms resting on the wood on either side of my head. Caging me in, maybe afraid I'll disappear.

"Did you miss me, Siren?" He asks. "Miss my cock stretching your pretty little pussy the way only I can?" My core clenches as he presses that appendage right where I need it most. Anticipating the stretch that borders on pain.

"You know I did." My blush is back in full force. Funny enough, it doesn't embarrass me anymore. This man makes me feel alive like no other.

Mac gently pulls me away from the door, settling us on his bed. His hard body surrounds my much smaller frame as he proceeds to reward my courage to go after exactly what I want.

***

Hours later, I greedily suck down the glass sweet cool lemonade as I recover from the best sex of my life. I lost count of the number of orgasms he wrung from me.

He finally took pity on my poor satiated body, letting me escape his bed for some rehydration. It took promises of more wicked delights to convince him to let me go even temporarily.

He may or may not have cinched my agreement with his mouth teasing between my legs, mindless as I chased his devilish mouth for the pressure I needed to fly over the edge of orgasm. The evil man withholding until I agreed.

Contentment settles all the way down to my bones as we quench our thirst, him with a beer and a glass of lemonade for me.

We're deep in discussion on the pros and cons of accepting Ryker's offer. My dream is at my fingertips. With a little help from the MC.

Mac is giving me the nudge I need to take a leap of faith, promising to be there to catch me if I fall. Mac's encouragement is all the reassurance I need.

I think I'll let him try "convincing" me a little longer before I confess I'm going to do it.

I definitely benefited from his attempts at persuasion in the bedroom earlier.

The clubhouse reached capacity while we were gone, standing room only now. Luckily, the brothers saved a stool for us at the bar.

Nothing can wipe the smile from my face as I survey the room snuggled comfortably against Mac's chest.

Only one dark cloud remains. Josie is nowhere in sight. She's been a fixture in the club when the brothers are partying, always right in the middle of the fun but not tonight.

Even though I'm suspicious her absence is related to Michael's "little birdie" comment, I don't ask. I have absolutely no desire to see harm come to her – if she truly *did* betray the club.

The brothers will handle it in their own way no matter my opinion. It's just the way things work in their world. A world I willingly walked into by loving Mac.

I don't think I want to know.

Demi's sudden appearance at the bar yanks me from my somber thoughts. She looks like a disappointed momma bear.

"Personally, I think you should've made him work harder for your forgiveness. Maybe a little begging on his knees first. But that's just me. If he's what you want, I'll keep my mouth shut. For now, anyway." From the wink accompanying her words, I know she isn't serious. At least not completely.

Giving me no time to respond, she turns her critical eye to survey the room before her exuberant shout sails to the rafters. "Shots!"

Why is it always shots with my friend? Guess she's looking for a good time tonight.

She shifts expectant eyes to me when not a single person takes the bait.

"Girl, I love you but I am *not* doing shots with you again. I learned my lesson at Dean's." Shaking my head, I decline with absolutely no regret.

Her disappointment in me is short lived as her eyes move to scan the room for her next victim. "Well, you're no fun. I need someone to do shots with me!"

Again, no one volunteers to join her spiral squad.

I suspect that's all Ryker's influence.

She zeroes in on Bomber, the serious brother has the misfortune of catching her eye during her sweep. "Bomber! Come do a shot with me."

Uh oh, this isn't going to end well.

Ryker appears out of nowhere, stepping between her and Bomber before he can even take a step in her direction. "Demi, what did I tell you about flirting with my brothers?"

He doesn't give her a chance to respond. In a flash, he advances right into her personal space, bending to put his shoulder to her stomach. He straightens with my friend draped over his broad shoulder.

Oh boy, I think his veins are about to pop out his temples.

My eyes, riveted by the fascinating spectacle of someone getting one over on my friend, follow their progress to the back of the clubhouse. I watch helplessly as her fists beat his back until they disappear.

"Put me down you Neanderthal! Remember what happened the last time you manhandled me?" As her voice fades, I turn to Mac for help.

But he's already shaking his head. "No, Siren. I am not getting involved in their drama. She played with fire, now she's gonna feel the burn."

Oh boy! I think my friend might be in over her head.

"Come on, baby. It's time for bed." With a look of sexual promise, Mac takes my hand for our own stroll back to his room.

Forget Demi. I've got my own kind of trouble on my hands.

And I couldn't be happier about it.

Epilogue

Kate

The car is packed – the new car Mac insisted April needed to start this new chapter of her life. There is nothing else to do to delay our departure.

As much as I've pushed April to pursue her dreams. To step out of her comfort zone and experience all the wonders life has to offer, now that the time has come, I can't seem to convince myself to let her go. Don't want to see her leave this home we've built together.

This is what is best for her. Logically, I know that. But tell that to my breaking heart, knowing she's not going to be there every morning. Not going to be there to watch trashy reality TV with me.

But I need to be strong. For her. For myself. This is what April needs.

I need to let go. Let her fly.

"Ready?" I lean back into the strong comfort of Mac's chest as his arms slide around my waist. His question a puff of hot air along the exposed column of my neck almost distracting me from my distress, always knowing exactly how to pull me out of a spiral.

What would I do without this man?

The last six months have been the best of my life. All thanks to the man at my back.

Once I finally let him in, he's been my rock. He's shown both April and me the kind of family we can have with him in the picture. I can't imagine my life without him. Luckily, I don't have to go down that dark road.

How on Earth I thought I could live without him is a mystery to me.

"I don't want to let her go." My words are muffled where I buried my face in his shirt. No doubt I'm leaving tears and snot all over him but he doesn't seem to care as he tightens his hold on me, pulling me closer. Being my rock as I navigate my conflicting emotions.

"Yes, you do. Siren, you've been pushing her to spread her wings. It's time to let your chick fly." Always the voice of reason, his words give me strength. I hang on for just another minute, drawing from his strength before straightening my spine.

You can do this.

Running out of the house with her last bag, a beautiful smile graces April's face along with a lightness that was missing until the last few months. She's blossomed under the careful watch of Mac and his MC family.

"That's everything!" The excitement in her voice a relief.

I'm not the only one Mac has helped overcome fears. The two have become close since I finally pulled my head out of my butt and admitted how I feel about him.

He's the older brother watching out for her. Giving her the nudge to try new things, always there to catch her if she falls. Watching their bond grow, in such a healthy fashion, has only reiterated that I made the right choice.

I watch them now as he takes her bag and maneuvers it into the car with the rest of the boxes she's taking to college.

This journey will be a new beginning for us all. Her at school, Mac and me taking the next step in our relationship. He has his own boxes packed and ready to move into the house when we return.

As we all settle into the car, Mac turns right down Main Street as we set off to April's new home for the next four years. The college a couple hours away gives her just enough space to expand her horizons. Close enough to come home when the need strikes. No matter what happens, she will *always* have a home with me. With *us.*

Mac's fingers twining with mine breaks me from my bittersweet thoughts as we merge onto the highway.

"Love you, Siren." His words are a whisper of his lips pressed to the back of my hand.

"Love you, too." I promise.

Life isn't perfect. This life is amazingly imperfect, but I wouldn't have it any other way.

And we're just getting started.

The End

Thank you so much for reading Mac's Choice! I really hope you loved Mac and Kate's story as much as I do! Want more of the Broken Soul's MC? Sign up[1] for my newsletter for a sneak peek at Demi and Ryker's story in Ryker's War. Pre-Order Ryker's War[2] today!

---

1. https://bookhip.com/SXRPGKX

2. https://books2read.com/RykersWar

About the Author

Dear Readers,

Thank you so much for reading my story! I hope you loved it as much as I love my couples as their stories come to life. It's not easy putting my thoughts and emotions into words and then sharing them with others. Knowing that you are out there enjoying my work makes it all worthwhile.

Like everything in life, this is a constant journey of growth, so please keep me honest.

Connect with me on Goodreads and Facebook to let me know what you think!

All the love

Terri Marie Pemberton

Read more at https://www.facebook.com/people/Terri-Marie-Pemberton-Author/61564954880361/.